Grimmtastic Girls

Red Riding Hood Gets Lost

Grimmtastic Girls

Grimmtastic Girls

Red Riding Hood Gets Lost

Joan Holub & Suzanne Williams

Scholastic Inc.

ISBN 978-0-545-51984-7

12 11 10 9 8 7 6 5 4 3 2 1   14 15 16 17 18 19/0

Printed in the U.S.A.   40
First printing, January 2014
Designed by Yaffa Jaskoll

To all the wonderful teachers who
encouraged in us a love of reading and books
throughout our childhood years.
~ J.H. & S.W.

Contents

It is written upon the wall of the Grimmstone Library:

Something E.V.I.L. this way comes.
To protect all that is born of fairy tale, folk tale, and nursery
rhyme magic, we have created the realm of Grimmlandia. In
the center of this realm, we have built two castles on opposite
ends of a Great Hall, which straddles the Once Upon River. And
this haven shall be forever known as Grimm Academy.

~ The brothers Grimm

1

The Audition

"Red Riding Hood?" The voice of Tom Thumb, Grimm Academy's drama instructor, cut through twelve-year-old Red's thoughts like a woodcutter's ax slicing into a willow tree.

Startled, Red dropped her Academy Handbook. *Thwap!* It hit the floor. The pages of the script she had tucked into it scattered.

It was Friday in third-period Drama class, and Red had been quietly rehearsing her scene as she waited backstage for her turn to audition. She was trying out for the lead role in the upcoming school play, *Red Robin Hood*. It was her first time auditioning for a play. But, hey — why not think big?

She would have auditioned for last year's play, too, but she'd been unable to fit Drama into her schedule until this term. Rule 56 in the Handbook: *You must be enrolled in Drama class to be eligible to try out for school plays.* Still, she'd been acting all of her life — even if it was only in private for family and friends.

Sweeping the script pages and handbook aside with one ankle-booted foot, Red hastily called out a reply through the blue stage curtain. "Coming!"

Her heart hammered inside her chest as she straightened her red cape squarely over her shoulders. Then she pushed her way through the heavy velvet curtains and stepped up to the front of the stage.

"Don't be nervous, don't be nervous, don't be nervous," she whispered to herself. The auditorium's acoustics were perfect, so anything she said in a normal voice onstage would be heard throughout the room.

Mr. Thumb, who was no bigger than . . . well . . . a *thumb*, hovered in the air only a couple of feet away from her face. He wore a hat made from an oak leaf, and a thistledown jacket that he was very proud of. It had been given to him by a fairy queen! Riding an iridescent orange and black monarch butterfly, he was a dramatic sight as he fluttered back and forth above the lights at the edge of the stage.

He'd come here once upon a time when Jacob and Wilhelm Grimm had founded the Grimm Academy, as well as the realm of Grimmlandia, as a safe place for all fairy-tale and nursery-rhyme characters to live.

Mr. Thumb and his butterfly buddy, Schmetterling (which was the German word for butterfly), were both actors who had traveled all over Grimmlandia before settling down to teach drama here at the Academy. They were famous!

After consulting the little vellum paper list he held in his tiny gloved hands, Mr. Thumb glanced up at Red. "You're auditioning for the lead? The role of Red Robin Hood?" His voice was as tiny as he was, so he used a silver thimble as a bullhorn to make himself heard.

"What a coincidence!" the butterfly exclaimed in a tinkly voice that reminded Red of wind chimes. "Her name's practically the same. Must mean she's meant for the role!"

Hope rose in Red, and she sent the butterfly a wobbly smile. Part of her Drama grade depended on her audition performance. But more than anything, she wanted that starring role. Acting was her dream. And like Schmetterling had said, the role of Red Robin Hood was *made* for her. She loved the character and was sure she could bring it to life, if only she was given the chance.

Mr. Thumb frowned at the butterfly. "Her name is not the same at all, Schmetterling! *She's* named Red *Riding* Hood. The character in our play is a girl named Red *Robin* Hood. Completely different."

The Drama instructor signaled someone in the back of the room. Red blinked as a spotlight as bright as a hundred candles suddenly found her.

"Ready when you are, Red," said Mr. Thumb.

"Good luck!" the butterfly told her. With that, the two of them zoomed offstage.

A waiting silence fell. Blinded by the spotlight, Red could see only dark shapes filling the auditorium seats. Those shapes were people. Some were students who'd already auditioned or would soon be auditioning. Would they compare her performance to their own? Judge her? How would she stack up?

"You can do this, you can do this, *youcandothis*," she muttered under her breath.

And she knew she could. Really. She was a drama-queen-and-a-half when it came to acting. Nothing made her happier than to act out bits from her favorite stories and plays for her BFFs, Rapunzel and Snow. Last night she'd even rehearsed her *Red Robin Hood* scene for her newest BFF, Cinda (short for Cinderella), who'd just started at the Academy this term.

Still, Red had never auditioned on a real stage before. In front of a big room full of people. Her hands and knees shook.

"Ready when you are," Mr. Thumb repeated from somewhere in the darkness beyond the stage lights.

"O-okay." Red's mouth felt as dry as an old leather trunk.

All at once, every single word she'd memorized flew out of her head as if riding away atop Schmetterling. How grimmensely frustrating! She knew this *Red Robin Hood* scene by heart! She'd practiced her lines so many times, she could almost recite them backward.

Seconds crawled by like hours. From the back of the room, one of the dark shapes coughed. The sound echoed throughout the auditorium. Red just stood there, feeling lost.

"I — um — I," she stammered.

Tendrils of her long, dark curly hair, which had glittery red streaks in it, were sticking to her forehead. The spotlight was making her hot and sweaty. Why, oh, why had she worn her cape? It was making her even hotter. Should she take it off?

As she reached to do just that, her stomach clenched. She'd only eaten a single bite of the knick-knack paddywhack pancake-stack Mistress Hagscorch had served for breakfast in the Great Hall that morning. Had that one bite made her sick? Or maybe she was simply too hungry to concentrate. Or too nervous.

"Red, are you okay?" It was Mr. Thumb's voice again.

"Sure. Fine. I —" But suddenly, she felt weirdly dizzy. She smiled brightly into the darkness. Then before she could finish her sentence, she crumpled onto the stage floor.

Thump!

Next thing she knew, she heard the hum of flapping wings close by. A bug was buzzing around her face. With her eyes still shut, she batted her hand at it. *Whack!*

"Whoa! Watch it!" a tinkly voice called out.

Red's brown eyes popped open just in time to see Mr. Thumb and Schmetterling whirl off in a spiral, surprised looks on their little faces. *Oops!* She'd smacked them away!

As she watched, Mr. Thumb lost his seat and began to fall. Luckily, Schmetterling recovered quickly and zoomed over. Mr. Thumb landed astride the butterfly.

"Wh-What happened?" Red asked, looking around woozily. She couldn't figure out why she was lying flat on her back on the wooden stage.

Slowly, she became aware of the circle of students around her. Their faces wore a mixture of concern and alarm as they stared down at her. How embarrassing that they were all seeing her like this, stretched out on the floor!

Not only that, they'd just seen her whack the teacher. A mistake like that couldn't be good for her Drama grade. But that paled in comparison to botching her audition!

Red tried to push herself up. Her arms were all tangled in her cape. Her entire top half was wrapped up like a red mummy.

Creak! Someone kneeled behind her on the stage and looped a strong arm around hers.

"Hey, I always thought you were a little dizzy, Crimson," a boy told her in a low voice as he helped her up to a sitting position. "You didn't have to faint to prove it."

Wolfgang? It had to be. That boy was always calling her by red synonyms instead of her real name. Which was *so* annoying. He'd started doing it last year when they'd had Calligraphy and Illuminated Manuscripts together. Apparently he'd noticed all the different names for shades of red ink. She was taking the class again this year, but not by choice. Her teacher had insisted on it since her penmanship was grimmtrocious.

Now that she was sitting up, Red fought her way out of her tangled cape. Then she looked over her shoulder at Wolfgang. She could hardly believe it! Mr. Anti-social — being nice? But there he was, a teasing grin lifting one side of his mouth.

"Name's Red," she mumbled. Of course he already knew that. They'd both been going to Grimm Academy since first grade.

Wolfgang's grin widened. Why had he helped her? He hardly spoke to anyone. Ever. He didn't show up at GA parties. He hadn't even attended the ball Prince Awesome had given at the Academy last weekend. He didn't have many friends. Probably because he mostly ignored everyone. Wolfgang seemed to prefer hanging out on his own in Neverwood Forest. Where anyone with half a brain "never would" go. Basically, he had a reputation as kind of a loner.

Still, in spite of all that, lots of students seemed in awe of him. Probably because he acted all cool and confident. The way Red wished she had acted a few minutes ago while trying to audition for this play.

In a hurry to put the whole episode behind her, Red leaped to her feet. She stumbled a little in her cape as she took a few steps forward.

Wolfgang to the rescue again. He stood and grasped her arm, steadying her. He was a lot taller than she was, so when he tilted his head down to look at her, a curtain of brown hair fell across his face. With a flick of his head he flipped it out of his pale gray eyes.

"You okay?" he asked. Although his eyes were teasing as always, he really did sound concerned. Or maybe he was pretending for some reason. After all, he was a gifted actor. In fact, he'd been grimmazing as the second lead in last year's play, *Peter and the Wolf*. Word was that he could shape-shift, too, though Red wasn't sure if anyone had ever actually seen him do it.

"Uh-huh," she replied. "I'm fine now." Still feeling embarrassed about her fainting episode, she snatched her arm free.

Immediately the friendly, teasing expression in Wolfgang's gray eyes faded. He tucked his fingers in his back pockets and hunched his shoulders. His head dropped forward, so that his hair shadowed his expression, and he took a few steps backward.

"Wait —" She took a half step in Wolfgang's direction. She should thank him. He'd been trying to be nice after all. And in her embarrassment, she'd been kind of rude in return.

"S'okay," he said. "Glad you're feeling better. See you, Scarlet." With that he ambled off, acting all casual like she hadn't hurt his feelings.

"Red! My name's Red," she corrected, frowning after him.

"Are you all right?" Mr. Thumb asked.

She looked over and saw that he and Schmetterling were hovering just out of reach. Probably afraid of getting accidentally whacked again.

Pushing her dark curls back, Red nodded. She wished the crowd of students around her would leave. The way they were staring made her feel like a bug under a magnifying glass. She caught Schmetterling's sympathetic glance. He could no doubt relate to that feeling!

"What do you think happened?" she heard someone whisper.

"Stage fright, I bet," a boy replied.

"Yeah, some people can't handle the pressure," said a girl with a British accent.

Red pretended she hadn't heard the comments. Though the first thing was true, she hoped the second one wasn't. She was no weakling!

"Sorry about fainting and about whacking you both," she apologized to Mr. Thumb and his butterfly. "It was a reflex action."

"No worries," said Schmetterling. "We've been booted out of enough theaters in the past to be accustomed to a certain amount of reject —"

"Ahem!" Mr. Thumb interrupted. "Apology accepted," he told Red.

She smiled, relieved, but she still couldn't believe what had just happened. She'd fainted. Failed her audition. What a nightmare! Acting had been her dream forever. But maybe she'd only been kidding herself. Her heart sank at the thought. Was it possible that she wasn't born to be on the stage, after all?

2

Wacky Basket

Bong! Red jumped a little as a low tone suddenly sounded from the Hickory Dickory Dock clock over in the Great Hall. The tone echoed throughout the school, signaling that it was eleven thirty. Lunchtime.

Looking around at the Drama students, Mr. Thumb held up his thimble bullhorn and announced, "That's it for auditions this period. We'll continue in class on Monday."

"But I thought you were going to post the official cast of actors this weekend," protested a girl named Polly. Red recognized her voice from a minute ago. She was the girl with the British accent who had suggested maybe Red couldn't handle the pressure of the audition. Polly drank a lot of tea and roomed in Ruby Tower in the same sixth-floor dorm as Red's friend Cinda's two stepsisters.

Mr. Thumb lifted his tiny eyebrows. "And now I've decided that I'll post them Monday after school instead," he informed Polly.

Schmetterling curved his antennae in the shape of question marks in her direction. "Do you have a problem with that?"

Polly's mouth pursed as though she'd just taken a sip of tea and discovered she'd put too much lemon in it. "No," she huffed. Her long blond hair was done up in a ponytail that swished from side to side when she shook her head. "It's not really fair, though. I would've gotten to read my scene today if not for *some* people!" Turning away, she and her perky ponytail swished offstage.

Although Polly hadn't even glanced at Red, everyone knew exactly who she was talking about. It was Red's fault the auditions had wound up running over to next week!

As students began to step down from the stage and file out of the auditorium, Red looked for Wolfgang again. She'd hoped he was still around so she could finally thank him. But it looked like he'd slipped away without her noticing. She went back for her handbook, which was still lying on the floor behind the curtain. Then she headed for the stage steps, too.

"I'll look forward to your do-over, Red," Mr. Thumb called to her from his perch atop Schmetterling.

"Huh? Oh, I don't know if I'll try out again," she replied, surprising herself. "Maybe I'll do scenery painting instead." *Why did I say that?* she instantly wondered. Her illuminations weren't much better than her calligraphy. Both pretty much stunk. She didn't care about art or fancy writing. She wanted to act!

"What? You've got talent! Don't be a giver-upper," Mr. Thumb encouraged.

"Um, okay, thanks. I'll think about it," said Red.

"And don't forget your basket," called the butterfly.

Red paused at the top of the steps and looked back over her shoulder. "Basket?" she repeated, confused.

But then she saw it. A cute little picnic basket. It was sitting on the floor near the place where she'd fainted. About the size of a bread box, the nut-brown wicker basket had a swirly design on either end, double handles, and a lid that hinged in the middle.

"It's not mine," Red told him, shaking her head. "Somebody else must have left it. See you Monday." She was in a hurry to get out of there so she could forget this class had ever happened!

As she started down the steps, she lifted her hand in a little farewell wave to the teacher and Schmetterling. Instantly, the basket whipped from the stage, launched itself at her, and looped its handles over the arm she'd held out to wave.

"Whoa!" she said, rocking back on her heels.

"A magic basket!" Mr. Thumb exclaimed.

"Or else a very big, odd-shaped magic bracelet," added Schmetterling.

"Either way — it's not mine," said Red, staring at the basket hanging from her wrist. After sliding it off her arm, she bent and set the basket on one of the steps. Then she kept on going.

It was nice of Mr. Thumb to offer her a second chance to audition, she mused as she reached the floor and started for the auditorium doors. But there was no way she would try out again on Monday. *Nuh-uh!* Today had been embarrassing enough. She couldn't risk humiliating herself again with a tied-up tongue or another fainting spell.

No, the thought of another audition made her want to throw up. Better just to take a bad grade and accept that some dreams weren't meant to be. No matter how much that hurt.

Knowing she wouldn't have to put herself through this ordeal again, Red expected to feel relief. But to her surprise sudden tears welled in her eyes. She'd wanted to act in a school play for, like, ever. Now it looked as though that wasn't going to happen. Giving up on her dream was going to be really hard!

Clomp. Clomp. Clomp.

At the odd sound, Red glanced over her shoulder. That basket! It was right behind her. It had hopped down the stairs and was following her like a lost puppy. And now, seeing that it had her attention, it started doing tricks, spinning around and clicking its two handles.

"Go away," she snapped, in no mood to be amused. "Go find whoever you belong to."

She sped up. Her cape whooshed behind her as she raced for the auditorium door. As she reached to push the door open, the basket zipped around her and slipped itself over her arm again.

"What do you think, Schmetterling?" she heard Mr. Thumb ask. "A misplaced magic basket or a magical charm?"

"My money's on magical charm," the butterfly replied. "And it seems to have chosen Red Riding Hood."

Because of the perfect acoustics, Red heard their voices as if they were standing next to her instead of hovering way behind her above the stage. She stopped in her tracks and stared at the basket in wonder, hardly noticing when the two teachers buzzed off, chatting about the auditions.

"Wow," she breathed. Could they be right? Was this basket really a magical charm? *Her* magical charm?

A thrill of excitement ran through her, chasing away her embarrassment over her flubbed audition. Like everyone at the Academy, she'd been hoping her whole life that a magic charm would someday claim her. But if this basket was hers, she couldn't help wondering why it had picked her moment of defeat to appear. Was it trying to make her feel better?

Whatever! It was an honor for a charm to choose you. Students waited *years* before it happened to them. Of her three BFFs, only Cinderella had received her magical charm so far — a pair of sparkly glass slippers.

Red pulled open the auditorium doors. She could hardly wait to get a look inside the basket. Would it hold jewels? Or maybe an enchanted antidote that would cure her of stage fright? A don't-be-scared diamond tiara? A magic have-a-wonderful-audition wand?

Or maybe it would contain an important message that had come through time from the Grimm brothers themselves!

The minute she stepped outside the doors into the fourth-floor hallway, Red set the basket down on the polished marble floor. Her heart thumped with excitement as she lifted the basket's lid. She looked inside. And discovered . . . a piece of vellum paper folded in half.

Growing more excited, she pulled the paper out and unfolded it. There were words written on it:

A tisket, a tasket. ____ ____ ____ ____ ____ ____.

A fill-in-the-blank sentence with missing words? It was kind of a letdown compared to jewels or a message from Jacob and Wilhelm Grimm, thought Red. And she already knew how the rest of the nursery rhyme went: "A tisket, a tasket. *A green and yellow basket.*" So what? She stuck the note back in the basket and huffed a breath that blew her bangs upward for a second.

"So, if you are a magic charm, what kind of magic do you *do* exactly?" she asked the basket. It gently bumped her knee and then did a little twirl on one of its bottom corners, but didn't reply. Of course, she didn't know of any magic charms that *could* talk.

Just then, Red heard boys' voices. Prince Awesome and Prince Foulsmell walked by and peered at her curiously. She sent them a weak smile. She probably did look weird kneeling in the hall talking to a basket.

After they passed, she dropped her Academy Handbook into the basket and closed the lid. Then she looped her arm through the wooden handles, stood, and hurried on. Time for lunch. She was starving!

She was halfway down the hall before she realized she was heading the opposite direction she'd intended to go. *Oh!* Why did she have to be cursed with such a terrible sense of direction? She was always losing her way in the halls at school! Reversing her steps, she made for the grand staircase on the girls' side of the Academy.

As she walked, Red kept sneaking peeks at the basket on her arm. It did feel somehow right dangling there. Could it really be her very own charm? Charms had magical powers that only the people they belonged to could unlock. If this basket truly was her charm, though, only time would tell what powers it had.

Once she made it to the first floor, she dashed to her trunker, which was like a locker. There, she pulled out the ornate key she wore on a chain around her neck. She poked it into the keyhole just below the little heart-shaped portrait of her painted on the trunker door. "Five, six, pick up sticks," she said.

Snick! Creak! In response to the rhyming code she'd chanted, the fancy leather trunk in front of her opened on its own. Like all the other trunks lining the walls in the hallway, it stood upended tallwise instead of flat on its bottom in the normal way of trunks. It was as tall as Red was and about eighteen inches wide. Its lid had opened outward like a door to reveal a coat hook and three shelves inside. Red set her GA Handbook on one of them.

She tried to put the basket inside, too, but it seemed to have a mind of its own. To her surprise, it leaped from her arms to the floor. Then it scooted down the corridor toward the Great Hall!

"Wait! Hold up, you wacky basket!" she yelled.

Pushing the trunker door shut, she turned the key in its lock and chanted the second half of her trunker combination all in a rush. "Seveneightlaythemstraight!" *Snick!* As the trunker locked itself, Red dashed down the hall after the basket.

She was in Pink Castle now, the side of Grimm Academy where the girls lived and had most of their classes. The walls she was passing were hung with tapestries showing lush and lovely scenes of feasts and pageantry. And every so often she passed a tall stone support column with figures of flowers, birds, and gargoyles carved on its top.

She caught up to the basket just as it went whirling into the Great Hall. "Gotcha!" she exclaimed, grabbing it with both hands.

Then she straightened and glanced around. Heads had turned toward her, faces staring in surprise at her dramatic entrance. Instead of getting all flustered at the attention as she had in her audition, Red simply looped the basket's handles over one arm and curtseyed grandly. Just as if she was an actor onstage, doing a curtain call after a fabulous performance in a play. Numerous students clapped and whistled, enjoying her ability to laugh at herself.

If only she could be this relaxed onstage! But the only time she seemed able to perform before a crowd was when she *wasn't* on a stage!

3

Lunch Talk

The majestic Great Hall — where meals were served and fancy balls were held — was at the center of Grimm Academy. Two stories high, the Hall straddled Once Upon River and connected the Academy's two magnificent castles, which stood one on either side of the river.

To the west of the river was Gray Castle, which was made of blue-gray stone. It was where Wolfgang and the other academy boys lived and had most of their classes. Pink Castle — the girls' side — stood east of the river. All the students' dorm rooms were located in the three turreted towers that topped each castle.

Like Red, everyone here was a character from literature. Some, like her BFF Snow White, were princesses (or princes). But others, including Red herself and her other two BFFs, were not. And though the four of them were named in the Books of Grimm, not everyone at GA was. Some came from other fairy-tale books or from nursery rhymes. Regardless, everyone in Grimmlandia had been brought here for safekeeping by the Grimm brothers.

Only recently had Red and her friends begun to realize what they needed to be kept safe *from*. Something really truly evil! An E.V.I.L. Society!

As Red headed for the lunch line, a girl with long candle-flame yellow hair called to her. She was seated at one of the two linen-draped tables that ran the entire length of the enormous two-story-high Hall. "Red! Over here! We got your lunch for you!"

It was Cinda. She, Rapunzel, and Snow were all sitting together. They'd saved Red a spot, too. And *uh-oh*. From the worried looks on the three Grimm girls' faces, she could guess that the news of her embarrassing fainting spell had already gotten around the Hall.

"Oh, hobwoggle," she mumbled under her breath. Because she really didn't want to talk about it.

Going over to the table, Red sat down in the empty space on the bench next to Cinda. Snow and Rapunzel were sitting across from them.

"Look at my new basket," Red began, trying to head off questions about what had happened at the audition. But her friends barely glanced at it. They were more concerned about *her*, and got right to the point.

"We heard you fainted," Cinda said, her blue eyes wide.

"Are you okay?" asked Snow as she re-pinned the bow that had slipped from her short ebony hair.

Red nodded. "Mm-hmm. Fine. So what's for lunch?" Peering at the others' plates she saw they were about half-way through eating.

Rapunzel slid one of the Hall's fancy silver lunch trays toward her. The delicate gold-rimmed white plate on it con-tained a serving of fig newt, a sour-eye scone, a mound of walldwarf salad, and a gingerbread house small enough to fit in the palm of Red's hand. All were specialties of Mistress Hagscorch, the Academy's Head Cook. Luckily, her food tasted way better than it sounded.

Red slipped the basket off her arm and set it under the bench so she could eat. "Thanks, you guys," she said, genu-inely touched. "I wasn't looking forward to standing in the lunch line." She dug into her fig newt. *Mmm — delicious!*

Lunch was kind of hard to enjoy with three pairs of eyes staring at her, waiting for an explanation. Still, Red didn't want to admit her stage fright, even to her friends. Instead she decided to pin the blame on some-thing else.

"I think maybe I fainted because I didn't eat enough breakfast this morning." She grinned, trying to lighten everyone's mood. "Or maybe I was allergic to Mistress Hagscorch's knick-knack paddy-whack pancakes."

"Allergic?" echoed Snow. Her emerald green eyes rounded with worry. "Oh, dear. I wonder what ingredient could have —"

Oops, bad move mentioning allergies, Red decided. Snow was allergic to various things, but especially to fruit. She could talk about the dangers of allergies all day.

"Or it might have been because I didn't get much sleep last night," Red added quickly. Which was true. Her roommate, Gretel, had had a nightmare just before dawn. She'd screamed, waking Red and mumbling something about Mistress Hagscorch's oven. Afterward, Red had been unable to get back to sleep.

"Why didn't you tell us you were auditioning for the play today?" Rapunzel asked. Her heavily-kohled dark eyes studied Red impatiently. She was dressed all in black, as usual. Even her hair was black and was so long it brushed the floor at times.

"Yeah, if we'd known, we could've helped you more on that scene you were practicing," said Cinda.

"Sorry, I just didn't — that is, I was just — too stressed out about it," Red admitted.

"Why?" asked Snow.

To buy some time while she considered how to answer, Red shoved a spoonful of walldwarf salad into her mouth. Then she gestured toward her lips, wordlessly indicating,

"Sorry, can't talk now!" As she chewed, she lifted her eyes to the arched windows that lined the Hall and gazed through them to the sparkling blue river waters far below. Most of the windows were propped open so birds could fly in and out of the Hall, crossing in from one side and flying back out the other.

"No reason I guess," she said finally, after swallowing the bite of salad. She didn't want to admit the truth. That some small part of her had feared failure and that she'd hoped her friends wouldn't find out about it if it happened. They knew she lived to act! And now they knew she'd been a flop at her tryout.

As if sensing she needed a change of subject, Red's new basket suddenly started banging around under the table.

"What in Grimmlandia?" exclaimed Rapunzel. She pushed aside the tablecloth and peeked under it, then looked over at Red. "Is that thing magic?"

Nodding, Red pulled the basket out by its handles and showed it off. "Mr. Thumb thinks it could be my charm," she said proudly.

Her friends gasped.

"Really? Wow!" said Rapunzel.

"I can't believe you didn't say anything about this till now!" said Snow at the same time.

"I tried to when I first sat down," Red protested. "Only you weren't paying any atten —"

"Do you know what it can do yet?" Cinda interrupted in excitement. When her glass slippers were on her feet, Cinda, who was usually a terrible dancer, could sway and twirl around a ballroom beautifully.

"Not yet," Red replied. "But I can't wait to find out!"

Then she told them how the basket had appeared in the auditorium. "I thought it must belong to someone else, but it attached itself to my arm when I tried to leave without it."

"You're so lucky," Snow exclaimed, her eyes alight with pleasure.

Rapunzel nodded, smiling. "I'm really, really happy for you."

"Me, too," said Cinda, giving her a hug. "Is there anything inside it?" Cinda's glass slippers had tiny words written inside them that read: *These glass slippers will convey, the magical power to lead the way.*

Red showed her friends the fill-in-the-blank letter. "The nursery rhyme goes: A tisket, a tasket. A green and yellow basket."

"Yeah, but that's only five words, and there are six blanks here," Rapunzel noted, pointing to the blanks. She cocked her head and a few strands of her hair glittered under the overhead lights. Like Red, she'd added streaks to her black hair, but Rapunzel's were a dazzling blue instead of a glittery red.

Red shrugged. "Whoever wrote the note must have miscounted the rhyme's missing words."

"Or maybe it's supposed to be 'A tisket, a tasket. A brown and white wicker basket' or something like that," said Cinda.

"It seems like the note's message should be more special, though," said Snow. "Like it should mean something, or be some kind of clue."

As they continued eating lunch, the four Grimm girls took turns guessing what the missing words might be. It seemed pretty hopeless.

"I give up," Cinda said finally. "There are a million words that could fit in those blanks." But a second later her face lit up. "Hey! That basket would be a perfect place to keep *a certain thing*. A certain thing that needs to be kept safe, if you know what I mean?" In case Red hadn't gotten the hint, Cinda pushed the edge of her cloak aside to reveal the tip of a tapestry that was rolled up underneath it.

But it wasn't just any tapestry. It was the mapestry — a two-foot square magical cloth tapestry embroidered with a map of Grimmlandia. Cinda had literally stumbled over it when her glass slippers had led her to where it was hidden under a loose floor tile — right here in the Great Hall — at Prince Awesome's ball last week.

After Red set the basket in her lap, Cinda looked around to make sure no one was watching. Then she slipped the mapestry into the basket.

"That's a relief," said Cinda. "I don't think anyone's guessed about that *certain thing* also known as '*You Know What,*' since it was wrapped in vellum paper when I found it. But the fewer chances we take with it being discovered, the better."

"Good point," said Rapunzel. "It's probably better that someone besides you keeps it for a while. If the E.V.I.L. Society knows about its existence and figures out you have it, they might try to steal it."

E.V.I.L. was an acronym for Exceptional Villains In Literature. Red doubted whether the members of the group truly were *exceptional*, but they apparently liked to think of themselves that way.

The Grimm girls had stumbled on the existence of the society about the same time they discovered the mapestry. It seemed that E.V.I.L. had been quite active until Grimmlandia was founded. After that, the group had mysteriously died out. Just why it had recently begun to operate again, the girls had no idea.

Cinda nodded. "Yeah. Maybe we can trade off from now on. Take turns guarding it."

Red lowered her voice. "Since I've got it now, let's meet in my room after school today, okay? To plan our little, um, trip tomorrow morning to look for the —"

"Shh," warned Rapunzel before Red could add the word *treasure*. The girls glanced around them, checking that none of the other students were listening in.

They hoped the mapestry might lead them to the long-lost Treasure of Grimmlandia. In fact, a few days ago, an embroidered *X* had appeared on the mapestry, atop what appeared to be a tiny embroidered cottage in the middle of a stitched representation of Neverwood Forest. And *X* marks the spot where treasure is found, right? However, none of them knew exactly what that treasure was, or *if* it really and truly even existed.

Snow frowned. "It's weird not knowing who we can trust around here. I don't like suspecting everyone."

"Well, Malorette and Odette are E.V.I.L. members, for sure," said Cinda. She peered down at the end of the table, where her two stepsisters sat.

Those three girls did not get along, Red knew. But that wasn't Cinda's fault. Her Steps were mean, and definitely evil! A week ago, Cinda had overheard them discussing the Society on the night of Prince Awesome's ball.

"Why are they hanging around with *Wolfgang* all of a sudden?" Cinda asked suddenly.

"Huh?" Red leaned out from the table to see what Cinda was looking at. Sure enough, Wolfgang was at Malorette and Odette's table! And those two girls were jabbering away to him like the three of them were best friends. Usually Cinda's Steps only paid attention to *princes* who went to the Academy. Wolfgang was not a prince.

Had the girls invited him to sit with them? Red wondered. Why else would he hang out with Cinda's awful stepsisters when there were plenty of other empty seats? Not that Red wanted him near her, of course. She could certainly use a break from all the nicknames he came up with.

When Wolfgang's head started to turn in Red's direction, she whipped around. Breaking off a chocolate tile from the little gingerbread house's roof, she popped it into her mouth. Had he seen her staring? She hoped not.

Rapunzel raised an eyebrow. "I say we add Wolfgang to our E.V.I.L. Society suspect list."

Really? thought Red. She could see why her friends might suspect him, since he was hobnobbing with the enemy. Wolfgang was annoying, yes. But evil? Red just couldn't see it.

Ta-ta-ta-*ta*-ta-ta-*tum*! Trumpets blared.

31

At the sound, everyone stopped talking and all eyes turned toward the balcony at the west end of the Hall, the end closest to Gray Castle.

There, on a wide, carved wooden shelf, sat the School Board — a row of five shiny iron knights' helmets, each topped by a decorative feather. The visors on the helmets began to open and shut as if they were speaking. Which they were.

"Attention, scholars! The principal of Grimm Academy will now address you!" their formal voices chorused.

Stomp! Stomp! Stomp! The gnome-like principal climbed up a small ladder to gaze upon the students in the Hall from the balcony above. Although Rumpelstiltskin was his name, no one dared call him that. It was against the rules in the GA Handbook. When Cinda had first gotten to the Academy and hadn't known any better, she'd said his name three times. Red shook her head, remembering. Big oops. The principal had flown into a rage and Cinda had almost wound up with scullery duty!

The nameplate on the principal's office door read simply: Principal R. But the GA students had all made up nicknames for him. Things they would never call him to his face! Red's favorite was Stiltsky. Wolfgang preferred the Rumpster. And Cinda had recently coined a good one — Grumpystiltskin.

Suddenly, the principal's voice rang out. "Due to the disappearance of an important artifact from the Grimmstone Library last week, we want everyone to be on the lookout for suspicious activity."

The Academy's Grimmstone Library was an amazing, enormous place that not only held books, but also boxes of weird things such as kisses, sneezes, and advice. Not to mention artifacts. Red especially loved the aisles where you could find the gowns and dancing slippers, which students could check out and wear whenever there was a ball. But you never knew where exactly to find the library. It moved around the Academy and you had to find a special doorknob to locate its door.

Red was always getting hopelessly turned around in the GA halls, even when she wasn't trying to find a constantly-roving room. Usually she tried to follow one of her friends to the library — it was much easier that way.

"We'll be tightening security," Principal Rumpelstiltskin went on. "And our belts! Because the missing artifact, Peter Peter Pumpkineater's pumpkin, contained the Seeds of Prosperity."

He thumped his fist on the balcony railing. "I didn't want to worry you all with this, but I think it's for the best that we all be on our guard against future thefts. I'm not exaggerating when I say that, without those seeds, there will be lean times ahead." With that, the principal turned and stomped back down his stepladder.

As everyone took their seats again, murmurs rose to a dull roar as the students discussed this startling news.

But Red just rolled her eyes and quipped, "He forgot to wish us a happily-ever-after school day."

Snow nodded. "Sounds like he doesn't think our future will have very many of those."

Cinda leaned across the table and whispered, "Do you think he knows about E.V.I.L.? Maybe we should tell him. And about the *You Know What*."

Rapunzel shook her head. "We dare not trust anyone, not even him."

Not even Principal R? If they couldn't trust him, who could they trust? wondered Red.

"I just wish we could help more," said Cinda.

"Well there's pretty much zero chance of getting the pumpkin back," said Red.

The pumpkin wasn't even *in* Grimmlandia anymore. With their own eyes the Grimm girls had watched it change into a carriage. They'd traced its route on the mapestry as it rolled into Neverwood Forest and disappeared over the wall that surrounded Grimmlandia. That wall protected Grimmlandia from the Dark Nothingterror beyond, a place no one had ever visited and lived to tell about, according to their History teacher, Mr. Hump-Dumpty.

"If and when we find the treasure, we'll give it to the Academy," said Rapunzel. "That'll solve everything. Until then . . ." She pressed her finger and thumb together and drew them across her lips. "We keep 'em zipped."

As her words died away, the enormous hickory-wood grandfather clock that stood in the balcony at the east end of the hall began to recite a rhyme:

"Hickory Dickory Dock,
the mouse ran up the clock.
The clock strikes noon.
Fourth period starts soon.
Hickory Dickory Dock."

During the rhyme, a mechanical mouse popped out of a little door in the clock's face. As the rhyme ended it signaled noon by squeaking twelve times in a row. The squeaks were followed by twelve loud bongs that echoed throughout the school.

Immediately, the bluebirds that had been flying in and out of the open windows on either side of the Hall during lunch dived down and picked up the silver food trays in their beaks.

"Hey, wait, I wasn't finished with dessert!" called Red. Reaching up, she managed to nab her half-eaten gingerbread house before the bluebirds carried her tray off. She munched on the rest of it as the girls hurried toward the Pink Castle end of the Great Hall to reach their trunkers.

As they rushed along Snow's expression turned thoughtful and she leaned over to Red, who was beside her. "You know, Mr. Hump-Dumpty said something in History class earlier this week that sparked an idea about that *You Know What* in your basket. I want to check it out, but I can't remember what —"

Abruptly, Snow clammed up. Red followed her friend's gaze and saw two teachers coming toward them. Ms. Queenharts, who taught Comportment, was bustling down the hall. But Red knew it was Ms. Wicked, walking regally next to her, that had caught Snow's eye. She was Snow's stepmom and taught Scrying, the art of using crystal balls and other reflective surfaces to predict the future.

Ms. Wicked smiled down at them as she drew near. She was slender and tall, with perfectly-styled black hair. It was piled high inside a tiara with points so sharp they looked like icicles. "Good afternoon, girls."

Ms. Wicked's high heels clicked to a stop as her gaze fell on Snow. She frowned with disapproval. "Snow, dear, where did you get that awful bow? And sparkles — again? That dress isn't your most becoming, sweetie. You look better in plain styles. We'll just have to banish that one from your closet, won't we?" she said before she walked on.

Snow nodded at her stepmother's back, having visibly wilted under her words. After pulling out the blue bow, she ran a hand over her already-smooth ebony hair and brushed an imaginary wrinkle from her skirt.

So it was edged with lace and had some sparkles along the hem? *So what?* thought Red. Why did Ms. Wicked have to pick on Snow like that? It was almost like she was jealous of Snow or something. Red gave Snow a quick hug, saying, "I think you look cute!" But Snow only shrugged and sent her a wobbly smile, still looking unsure.

Meanwhile, Ms. Queenharts went scurrying down the hall after a student who'd broken a rule. "Off with your head! Off with your head!" she shouted. For someone who taught manners, she didn't really seem to have any of her own.

Rapunzel gazed after the two teachers. "Do you think any *teachers* could be members of the Society?" Though she didn't name anyone, possibly for fear of offending Snow, Red guessed she was thinking of Ms. Wicked.

Though Ms. Wicked acted nice most of the time, it was a niceness you didn't feel you could trust. Her smiles never seemed to reach her eyes. And the way she treated Snow made Red hopping mad! Though Snow's stepmom oozed sweetness to everyone else, she never missed a chance to put Snow down, especially when it came to her appearance and wardrobe.

There was just something sneaky and kind of, well, *wicked* about Ms. Wicked. Prime traits for a member of E.V.I.L., in Red's opinion!

Just then an announcement from the helmet-head School Board members sounded up and down the halls, broadcasting through the small vents set into the castle walls here and there. "Peter Piper, please report to the office to pick up the peck of pickled peppers your parents posted," they chorused.

The boy in question zoomed down the hall past the Grimm girls and hurried toward the Pink Castle grand staircase, heading for the fourth-floor offices.

"Don't forget. Secret meeting. My room. After school," Red reminded her friends.

4
Crystal Balls

After the Grimm girls finished up at their trunkers, Snow waved bye and rushed off. She was returning to the Great Hall for Balls class, taught by members of the Twelve Dancing Princesses performance troop. Meanwhile, Cinda, Red, and Rapunzel went along the first-floor Pink Castle hallway to their fourth-period classes. Cinda and Rapunzel both had The Grimm History of Barbarians and Dastardlies with Mr. Hump-Dumpty now.

Red was right next door in Scrying with Ms. Wicked. Learning to predict future events was pretty fun, actually. If someone other than the sneaky Ms. Wicked had been the teacher, it might have been one of her favorite classes.

Oh, no! Just as Red was about to step inside the classroom, she suddenly remembered something. She'd left the magic basket sitting under the lunch table. With the map-estry inside!

She was about to go back for it when she heard shrieks and gasps behind her. Whipping around, she saw the basket coming along the hall toward her. It was darting here and there along the floor, whirling around students' legs, and nearly causing some to trip as it headed in Red's direction. When it finally reached her, the basket leaped into her arms.

"Down, boy," said Red, trying not to laugh at its antics. "Sorry!" she called to the disgruntled kids it had annoyed on its way to find her.

Quickly, she lifted its lid a couple of inches and peeked inside. The mapestry was still there! Thank grimmness!

"What a cunning little basket," said an intrigued voice. Ms. Wicked had been standing right behind her. And apparently she'd noticed that the basket had been moving by magic. "Where did it come from?"

"I — um — I found it," Red said. She immediately regretted her truthfulness when Ms. Wicked's dark eyes began to glitter with even deeper interest.

"— at Old Mother Hubbard's Cupboard," Red quickly lied. The Cupboard was a small market tucked into a corner of the school on the fourth floor of the Academy where the offices and stuff were. Students could buy school supplies like shaped erasers, vellum paper, or village newspapers from all around Grimmlandia there, as well as a variety of other items.

At her reply, Ms. Wicked's eyes lost a little of their shine. Still, she smiled one of her wide fake smiles. "May I see it, please?" she asked, reaching for the basket. As if sensing the teacher's evil nature, the basket swung away, slid off Red's arm, and dropped to the floor. Then it skittered across the room, dodging students' feet to park itself right beside the square table Red shared with three other students, one on each side. How had it known which table was hers?

"It's shy," Red told Ms. Wicked with a weak grin. Then she ducked past her teacher into the classroom and quickly took her seat. But Ms. Wicked wouldn't be put off that easily. A few seconds later, her high heels clicked smartly on the stone floor as she came up beside Red's chair.

Before she could speak, Wolfgang, who was the only boy in Scrying class, dropped his handbook on the table and slung himself into his seat next to Red's.

"Got a question for you, Ms. W," he announced. "About the nature of reflective scrying."

"Oh?" Ms. Wicked turned to look at him, finally distracted from the basket. She seemed to genuinely like Wolfgang — yet another reason he probably deserved a spot on the Grimm girls' E.V.I.L. Society suspect list. Unfortunately.

Glancing sideways at Red, Wolfgang gave her a sly smile that she wasn't sure how to interpret. Then he reached into his jacket pocket and drew out a silver spoon with a swirly GA logo etched on the end of its handle. It was just like the ones used for every meal in the Great Hall, so Red guessed that that was where it had come from. She had a feeling there was a rule in their handbook against borrowing academy silverware, but it would be typical of him to break such a rule without thinking twice.

Wolfgang held the spoon out to Ms. Wicked, who took it but gave him a puzzled look.

"You're always telling us that a scrying object can be anything that reflects," he said. "So I wondered if a spoon would work."

"I suppose," Ms. Wicked said, turning the spoon over in her hand. "Though it would be a rather mundane choice. And it would have to be imbued with magic by its maker, of course."

"Of course," Wolfgang agreed amiably. "But here's what I was really wondering about. If you looked into the bowl of a magic spoon everything would appear upside-down because of the concave surface, right? Since upside-down is the reverse of right-side-up, does that mean you'd see into the past instead of the future?"

"Hmm, interesting notion," said Ms. Wicked. "However, not a very useful one. It's much more worthwhile to know the future, don't you think? After all, what's past is past. And the past is already written."

"True," said Wolfgang. "Only sometimes it might be useful — even *necessary* — for a lost or forgotten part of the past to be brought to light again. Right?"

At this, Ms. Wicked smiled in a slow, crafty, evil kind of way. "Possibly. It's time for class to start now. However, we can continue this conversation later. Why don't you stay a few minutes after class? I have fifth period free."

Wolfgang hesitated briefly, but then he nodded.

"What was that all about?" Red whispered to him as Ms. Wicked clicked her way back to the front of the room. Red didn't want to believe that Wolfgang was evil, but why did he keep acting all friendly with evil people? Was that stuff about the *forgotten past* a reference to E.V.I.L.? Of course, she couldn't exactly ask him, not without admitting she knew about that society herself.

"Nothing much," Wolfgang replied lightly. His gray eyes fell to the basket on the floor by her feet. "Magic charm?" he asked her.

"Maybe," she said, uncertain how much to tell him. "I'm not sure, but it *has* been following me around."

At this information, he leaned closer. "If I were you, I'd keep an eye on that basket."

"Why? What do you think it's going to do?"

"Oh, I don't know." He shrugged and shifted away again, as if he wasn't that interested anymore. His gray eyes flicked to Ms. Wicked and then back to Red. "Magic charms can be tricky, you know, if they end up in the wrong hands."

Although Red could think of a million questions she'd like to ask him about that statement, they were forced to stop talking as class began.

Ms. Wicked passed out crystal balls to everyone in the room and they began to practice with them. Even though Red had no plans to audition for the play again, she wished she could use her ball to find out what would happen at the Drama tryouts on Monday.

But the balls used in class weren't very powerful. They could only see partway into the next hour. Today, students were tasked with trying to extend their balls' prophecy range as much as possible. Which wasn't easy. The room rang with voices as everyone began coaxing their crystal balls to reveal the future.

Looking into her ball, Red assumed a dramatic and formal tone. "Oh, most revered and honored magic crystal ball," she began, spreading her arms wide before bringing her hands together to clasp them over her heart. "Wilt thou reveal the grade I attained on my Calligraphy test?" It wasn't at all necessary to speak to a crystal ball in a fancy way. Red just did it for fun.

She had Calligraphy and Illuminated Manuscripts fifth period, and graded tests would be returned to students today. She knew that her teacher, Peter Pen, was always hoping to awaken in her a love of hand lettering. But it was a hopeless task. The illustrated manuscripts, birthday announcements, and invitations to balls she practiced creating in class with quill pens and horsehair brushes were barely readable and splattered with ink stains.

"Verily, I don't think buttering up your ball will change your grade," quipped Wolfgang, imitating her formal language and tone.

Red laughed. She hadn't expected him to overhear her since the room was so noisy. Squinting, she tried to make out the letter grade at the top of the Calligraphy paper in the image that now swirled inside her ball.

"So what did you get?" Wolfgang asked a few seconds later. "Gradewise."

"It's kind of fuzzy," she hedged. Calligraphy was her worst subject and she was reluctant to tell him the grade she'd just seen.

"What, your ball or your calligraphy?"

"Both," she admitted. Then she sighed. "I got a C minus."

"Ouch," he said, wincing in sympathy.

She nodded. "Speaking of ouches, thanks for your help in Drama," she told him. "How'd you like my audition for the role of a falling tree?"

Now it was Wolfgang's turn to laugh. "You're not the only one around here with stage fright. I almost fainted at an audition once."

"You? No way!" Red said in surprise. "I saw you in last year's play. You were really good!"

Wolfgang shrugged off her praise, then studied her for a second, his light gray eyes peering into her dark brown ones. "Stage fright is a common problem for actors. I've just learned a few tricks to keep it under control."

Red was about to ask him what those tricks were when her basket surprised her by hopping into her lap. She looked up and saw the teacher approaching. "Uh-oh. Something Wicked this way comes!" she whispered. "Look busy."

Wolfgang bowed his head reverently toward his ball. "Oh, great and powerful ball," he began, in an obvious imitation of Red. "Wilt the period end before Ms. Wicked can reach the side of the Girl Who Falls Like a Tree?" He'd spoken quietly, so the teacher wouldn't hear.

Grinning over the way he'd twisted her words into a new nickname, Red glanced at the hourglass perched on a shelf at the front of the room. Judging from the amount of sand left in the top half, there were still at least six more minutes of class time to go. Her eyes flicked from the hourglass to Ms. Wicked, who was only two tables away by now. She hugged her basket close.

"Never fear. Saved by the ball," Wolfgang murmured, peering into his crystal ball. "*Fireball* that is."

"Huh?" Just as Red's eyes flicked to him, someone on the other side of the room gave a shout.

"Help! Fireball! I mean, my ball is on fire!" It was Polly, the girl who'd been so snippy to Red at the disastrous auditions.

"Move back!" yelled Ms. Wicked. Switching directions, she raced to the girl's side. But already the flames that had been leaping from the ball were dying away.

"Did you spill something on it?" Ms. Wicked demanded to know. She gestured a hand with long red-polished fingernails toward a china cup the girl held.

"Only a little tea," Polly said, sounding a bit defensive.

Frowning, Ms. Wicked pointed to a large mirror she'd hung on the wall at the front of the classroom. "Mirror, mirror, what's my rule?" she called out to it.

In response, words magically drew themselves in red lipstick upon the surface of the mirror. The whole class dutifully read them aloud:

47

"Bring food to class never.
Nor any drink whatsoever."

As Ms. Wicked went back to scolding a very pink-faced Polly, the sand in the hourglass ran out. Immediately, the hourglass rose into the air and flipped itself over to start again, ready for the next period.

Ms. Wicked abruptly ended her lecture. "Clear any remaining visions in your crystal balls, wipe down finger-prints, and leave the balls on your desks," she called out to the class. "Sixth period will be using them, too."

Quickly doing as instructed, Red then grabbed her bas-ket, twirled her cape over her shoulders, and zoomed off before the teacher could remember she'd been coming over to speak with her. "Nice work. With your crystal ball pre-diction, I mean," Red told Wolfgang as she followed him to the door. "One of those balls would've come in handy before my audition. It might've predicted my flubbing and faint-ing, so I could've stopped it from happening."

"Yeah. But what if, knowing what was coming, you'd avoided the audition altogether?" he asked as they left the classroom. "Then I would've lost my chance to play the hero!" His gray eyes sparkled with humor.

Red blinked. Hey, he was . . . cute! Why hadn't she ever noticed before?

Out in the hall, he dropped back a step to walk beside her. "So getting back to the future, want to get together later? After dinner, I mean? We could go over your lines. Prepare you for your second audition."

When she hesitated, Wolfgang pulled the spoon from his pocket. Holding it close to his face, he pretended to speak to it. "Oh great and powerful spoon, what will Burgundy say? Yea or nay?"

"My name's Red," she reminded him for the grimmillionth time, though she couldn't help laughing at his antics. Because this standoffish guy was actually funny! Wolfgang might occasionally be annoying, but he also intrigued her. She kind of would like to hang out with him, she decided. But then she remembered she'd already made plans.

"I can't," she said. "I'm working on a . . . a project with my friends tonight."

Wolfgang paused and looked back toward Ms. Wicked's door. Then he stopped walking and pulled Red over to stand to one side of the hall. "Tomorrow, then?"

"Oh, well, tomorrow we're all going to um . . . pick wildflowers." The lie was a lame one, but she couldn't tell him about the mapestry. The girls had agreed to keep it and their hunt for treasure a secret. Just like they'd agreed not to talk to anyone else at school about E.V.I.L.

"Where and when?" Wolfgang asked, interrupting her

thoughts. His tone was light, but Red sensed something concealed beneath it. Was it hurt? He wouldn't be asking so many questions unless he'd seen through her lie. He must be thinking she was trying to ditch him!

"Where and when what? Oh, the flower picking you mean? I'm not sure," she hedged. Since it seemed that he was going to keep pressing her for a time they could practice together, Red finally blurted out the truth. "Okay, if you must know, I'm not going to audition on Monday. Or ever."

"What?" He looked shocked, which embarrassed her for some reason.

She didn't need his disapproval. She could make her own decisions. "I'm not auditioning, okay? Give it up. Take a hint, why don't you?"

His eyes narrowed. "Oh, I never give up, Carmine. But I *can* take a hint. See you." Then he turned and went back down the hall — to go talk to Ms. Wicked about spoon predictions, no doubt.

Red hurried off in the other direction, worrying that she'd hurt his feelings, which made her feel horrible. So horrible that she hadn't remembered to remind him again that her name was Red. She spun around and called after him, "Wait! I didn't mean —" But her words were drowned out when some girls close by began to shriek with laughter.

She looked down to see that the basket on her arm was flapping its lid as if trying to soothe Wolfgang's feelings, too.

"Stop that, you wacky basket!" Red scolded. Unwilling to leave things so unsettled and hoping to explain herself more, she went back to the door of Ms. Wicked's classroom. However, she stopped short just outside, when she heard voices.

". . . seems pretty attached to her," Red heard Wolfgang saying doubtfully.

"You'll find a way. That basket is exactly what the Society needs! And you'll get hold of it for us, if you know what's good for you," Ms. Wicked replied.

Red gasped, backing away from the door in horror. Wolfgang must be part of E.V.I.L., after all — and he was planning to steal her magic basket!

Just let him try, she thought. Dashing off, she made her way to Calligraphy class, hugging her basket protectively under one arm.

5

Crumbs

After school Red took the twisty staircase up to Pearl Tower, one of the three towers — or turrets — at the top of Pink Castle. The other two turrets had jewel names, too, Ruby Tower and Emerald Tower. Over on the other end of the Academy at Gray Castle the boys' turrets were named Onyx, Topaz, and Zircon.

The winding stairs dead-ended on the sixth floor at a pair of doors. The emerald green one led to Emerald Tower and the pearly white one to Pearl Tower, of course. All the turrets had two floors and were connected by stone walkways. Getting around the Academy was so confusing that it had taken her all the way to the end of first grade to stop getting lost on her way up here.

Red opened the white door and stepped outside onto the stone walkway that ran between the towers. Ahead, the pointy roof of Pearl Tower gleamed a pale frosty white against a cloudless blue sky.

Hearing splashing water, Red peeked over the edge of the walkway to admire the new mermaid statue below. Cinda's roommate Mermily had recently added it atop the fountain on the fifth-floor patio. The statue was curved in the shape of an *S* and spurted water in streams that looped over each other and glistened in the sunlight before tumbling back into the lower rings of the fountain.

Down at the far end of the walkway, Red opened another pearly white door and entered the Pearl Tower dorm. She crossed the common area in the center of the tower, where the girls could hang out by a huge fireplace, sit in comfy, overstuffed chairs, or play games at a table.

Ringed around the common area, all along the inside of the tower wall, were numerous small alcove bedrooms. Red headed for the one she shared with Gretel. Cinda and Snow both roomed here in this dorm, too, with other alcovemates. But because she had a fear of heights, Rapunzel preferred the dungeon. She avoided the towers as much as possible, seldom climbing above the third floor.

The minute Red pushed back the curtain to enter her alcove, she immediately spotted the crumbs on the floor. They led straight to a pair of legs dangling over the edge of the very high canopy bed on the opposite side of the room from Red's.

"Oh, hi!" Red said, surprised. She hadn't expected Gretel to be in. The other three Grimm girls were coming here for their meeting soon. If Gretel stuck around, they'd have to find somewhere more private. Although Gretel was about as likely to be a member of E.V.I.L. as a smiley-face sticker was, Red couldn't very well tell her about the mapestry, the treasure, and the E.V.I.L. Society since she and her friends had sworn to keep those things secret.

At the sound of Red's voice, Gretel sat up. She'd woven her brown hair into a thick braid that hung forward over one shoulder and almost reached her waist. There was an open book in her lap titled *Trails and Hikes Around Grimmlandia*. Gretel was totally into hiking. And into something else, too: snacking and being messy about it.

Red felt the tiny crumbs crunching under her ankle boots as she crossed the room. She set her basket on the desk that was tucked under her loft bed across from Gretel's.

Looking up from her book, Gretel's quick brown eyes immediately went to the basket. "Where'd you get that?"

"It just appeared during Drama," Red told her "And it seems to want to be mine."

"Ooh! You got a charm!" Gretel began bouncing on her bed.

"Not so fast," said Red. "I *think* it's my charm, but I'm not one hundred percent sure yet."

Gretel scrambled down the ladder at the end of her bed and came to examine the basket. Remembering that *You Know What* was hidden inside it, Red worried she might try to open it. Sure enough, Gretel did try. However, the basket held both sides of its hinged lid tightly shut, not letting her see the mapestry inside!

"It doesn't open," said Gretel, sounding disappointed.

Red breathed a silent sigh of relief. "Sometimes it does." Remembering what she'd told Ms. Wicked about it, she said, "Maybe it's just feeling shy or something." She hated keeping secrets from Gretel, but that was the way it had to be, at least for now.

"So have you discovered what it can do yet?"

As Red shook her head, Gretel pulled a cookie out of her skirt pocket and took a big bite. Red glanced down at the floor, where more crumbs fell as Gretel munched. Raising her eyebrows, she looked back up at her roommate. Then she pointed down at the crumbs on the floor.

"Oops! Sorry. But cookies are crumbly, what can I say?" said Gretel.

Red sighed inwardly. Gretel always managed to leave a trail of crumbs no matter what she was eating! Still, Red didn't want to be mean about it. Then she looked more closely at the half-eaten cookie still in her roomie's hand.

"Hey, is that one of the oatmeal cookies I baked yesterday?"

Gretel popped the last of the cookie into her mouth and dusted her hands. More crumbs drifted to the floor. "Yuh uhn thur vur nummy." She finished chewing, then repeated, "I mean, yes and they're very yummy!"

Both girls giggled.

On the first day of the term, all students at the Academy had been assigned a tower task — a small job they were responsible for doing. Cinda was Hearthkeeper. Snow was Tidy-upper. No one knew what Rapunzel's job was because she kept mum about it. Gretel was Pathfinder, which meant she helped anyone in the dorm who wasn't getting along to find a path toward friendship.

It was Red's job as Snackmaker to keep the cookie jar full in Pearl Tower's common room, which was fine with her. She loved baking! And unlike some other students, Red got along great with the Academy's head cook, Mistress Hagscorch. Still, lately she'd noticed that cookies had been disappearing from the jar at such an alarmingly fast rate that she was having to bake twice as often as usual.

"How many have you had?" Red asked her roommate suspiciously.

Gretel thought for a minute. "Well, I ate three for breakfast, five for lunch, and just now I had two more for a snack." She paused. "And I've got seven more saved for dinner tonight."

Red stared at her. "Do you mean you've eaten nothing but cookies all day today?"

"Since school started last week, actually," Gretel admitted sheepishly. "Oatmeal's good for you, though, right?"

"Yeah, but . . . wait. Is this because of those nightmares you've been having?" Red guessed. "The ones that always start with you doing scullery duty for Mistress Hagscorch in the kitchen below the Great Hall?"

Gretel's eyes went wide and she nodded vigorously, causing her thick brown braid to bounce up and down. "Uh-huh."

"And then she sneaks up behind you while you're starting to bake loaves of bread. And then she pushes you into the ov —" said Red.

"Stop! Don't say it." Shivering, Gretel wrapped her arms around herself. Then she said in a tiny voice, "I can't go back to the Great Hall ever again. If I do, I'm toast! Literally. Pushed into the oven to bake with the bread. I just know it!"

"Calm down," Red soothed, giving her a quick hug. "I know Mistress Hagscorch is always talking about fattening students up, but that's only because she likes to see people enjoy her food. Not because —"

"— she plans to fatten us up for *her* dinner?" finished Gretel. "Are you sure? Because I'm not."

"Don't you miss hanging out with everyone during meals?" Red coaxed in a singsong voice. "You can't live on cookies, you know. And you can't let fear keep you from eating healthy food." *Or from both of us getting a good night's sleep*, she almost added. She didn't, though. It wasn't Gretel's fault that she was having nightmares!

Gretel shrugged. "I know. But all that isn't worth taking a chance of becoming Gretel Pie, thank you very much."

Red could see how unhappy Gretel was. But how could she demand that Gretel face her fears when Red couldn't face her own? After all, hadn't she decided to let her stage fright keep her from her dream of acting in the school play?

Going over to the doorway, Red peeked out into the common room. No sign of her other friends yet. She ran her fingers over the alcove's white velvet curtain, which was studded with shiny seed pearls. She really wanted to help Gretel, but . . .

"Hey, do you smell smoke?" Gretel asked suddenly.

Red's eyes rounded as she sniffed the air. Then she and Gretel ran to the window of their room and gazed outside.

Down below, Principal R was at his alchemy experiments again, trying to turn yet another object into gold. This time it was the statue of himself that stood in the center of Maze Island.

It looked to Red like his experiment was turning into a disaster. One of the maze's hedges was ablaze. "Great grimmfire!" she whispered.

"Oh, no!" moaned Gretel. "Why doesn't he just give it up?"

The fact that no one had ever succeeded at alchemy hadn't yet stopped Principal R from trying. And he'd somehow convinced his dragon-lady office assistant, Ms. Jabberwocky, to help out with his doomed experiments.

As Red and Gretel watched, Ms. Jabberwocky beat out the hedge fire with her long green tail. At the same time, she tossed a small object into the air with a clawed hand. Tilting her head back, she opened her mouth and chomped the object when it dropped in.

It was probably a spicy jalapeño pepper, Red figured. That's what she usually ate when she was helping with Stiltsky's experiments.

Hearing a noise behind them, Red turned from the window to see the alcove's curtain wiggling. "Knock, knock," Cinda called from beyond it.

"Come in," Red called back. Cinda and Snow slipped into

the room to join Red and Gretel at the window. They all four stared down at the maze.

"Now!" hollered the principal. Ms. Jabberwocky let out a blast of orange breath-fire to heat the statue.

"Is Principal R really trying to turn his own statue into gold?" asked Cinda.

"Looks like it," said Red.

"This is nuts!" said Gretel.

As usual, things went awry. There was an explosion. Then the wooden benches surrounding the statue caught fire. Flames and smoke rose up from the center of the maze, and alarms went off all over the school.

Jack and Jill, a pair of twins who attended the Academy, sprang to the rescue. Swinging their magic pail between them, they raced from the school up a small hill and down it again to Once Upon River.

Quickly, they hopped aboard one of the swan-shaped boats docked along the shore and zoomed over to Maze Island. After chanting a few magic words, they tossed their pail into the air. As it tumbled down into the river, it grew bigger and bigger until it was as large as the boat itself!

Dunk! The gigantic pail sunk, scooping up an enormous amount of water, then rose into the air over the center of the island. It dumped its load. *Splash!* And just like that, the fire was out. Unfortunately, the principal and Ms. Jabberwocky also got sopping wet, which made the principal grimmighty angry!

"Yikes. Here we go again," Snow said to the other girls in a half-amused, half-concerned voice.

Sure enough, Principal R began hopping up and down like a cricket and yelling at the statue he'd just set afire. Like it was the statue's fault that it was partly melted now! He even climbed up on the pedestal to hammer the statue with his fists. That turned out to be a mistake. Suddenly, he slipped in water the pail had dumped. Waving his arms around and around, he spun a few times, wobbled, and then toppled right off the pedestal into the maze of hedges.

"Uh-oh," said Cinda. "Hope he can find his way out."

"Yeah," said Red. "I never can. That maze is crazy hard unless you have help."

By now, a bunch of other kids had come outside to watch the spectacle from shore. Some called out directions to help the principal escape the maze.

"I'm going down there!" Gretel announced.

As Gretel headed out of their room, Red noticed that she grabbed another cookie from the stash she was keeping at her desk. She obviously hadn't taken to heart anything Red had said.

"Rapunzel bailed on us," Cinda said once Gretel was gone. "She wants us to fill her in on our discussion at dinner."

"Okay," said Red. She didn't ask why Rapunzel had bailed. They all knew her fear of heights had everything to do with it. Letting fear stop you from doing what you wanted to do was something Red totally understood better than ever after her botched audition!

Suddenly, a pleased look came over Snow's face, and she snapped her fingers. "I just remembered something I wanted to check out. It has to do with the mapestry." She turned toward Red. "Can I see your handbook?"

"Sure." Red fetched it from her basket. Though the lid hadn't opened for Gretel, it opened for *her*, no problem. Was that a clue that the basket really must be her charm?

"What do you want to look up?" she asked Snow.

"Try biographies of famous Grimmlandiers," Snow replied. "In our history text."

All of their school subjects were contained in one GA Handbook, but not all at once. You had to ask your book for whatever subject you wanted before opening it. And since handbooks only worked properly for their owners, Red pressed the oval on the cover of hers. "The Grimm History of Barbarians and Dastardlies," she instructed. Then she handed the book to Snow.

Snow thumbed through the contents page. "Here it is." She pressed her fingertip over a chapter heading. After the book magically flipped open to the chapter she'd chosen, she skimmed through to find what she was looking for.

"Aha!" she said after a minute. Then she read aloud from a page: "Grandmother Enchantress is the most ancient and powerful enchantress in all of Grimmlandia."

"So?" asked Cinda. "That's not exactly news. Grandmother Enchantress is legendary!"

Red shot Snow a puzzled look. "Yeah, I don't get what she has to do with the mapestry."

"Wait," said Snow, resting the book on the windowsill. With an eager look on her face, she ran a fingertip over the words "Grandmother Enchantress." Instantly, a small, transparent bubble rose to hover a few inches above the page. Inside it were further choices: *Early Childhood, School Years, Achievements.*

Snow studied the choices, then poked her finger at the words *Early Childhood. Pop!* The bubble popped, disappearing the second she'd made her choice.

As Snow skimmed the Early Childhood page that appeared, a triumphant look came into her green eyes.

"Listen to this!" she said to Cinda and Red. "Grandmother Enchantress still resides where she was born — in a cottage at the center of Neverwood Forest."

Closing the Handbook with a satisfied snap, she gave it back to Red. "I remember Mr. Hump-Dumpty saying she was born in Neverwood. Get it? Her cottage must be the one embroidered on the mapestry! By the *X* where the mapestry wants us to go!"

"You think Grandmother Enchantress has the treasure?" Cinda asked. "And that she'll let us have it to help the Academy?"

"I don't know," said Snow. "I just have a feeling that the mapestry is directing us to her cottage!"

"Wish we knew for sure that there really *is* a treasure. And what it is exactly," said Red.

"Gold and jewels," insisted Snow, who adored sparkly things. "What else would it be?"

"Nothing in the old legend mentions gold or jewels or anything else, though," Red noted as she went over to set her book on her desk. Seeing the vellum note lying in her basket, she took it out and slipped it inside her handbook for safekeeping.

"No need to," said Snow. "Everyone knows the equation."

"Equation?" Red asked blankly.

Snow grinned. "Gold plus jewels equals treasure, of course!"

The three Grimm girls laughed.

"I hope you're right," said Cinda.

"Me, too," said Red. "Anyway, we'll find out soon enough. Maybe even tomorrow!"

6

Neverwood Forest

That night Red was jerked from sleep by another of Gretel's middle-of-the-night screams. "Gretel, wake up!" she called across the room. She heard murmurs from the rooms on either side of theirs and realized she wasn't the only one Gretel had woken.

"Huh? Wha —" Gretel said groggily. "Did I scream? Sorry."

Red sat up in bed. "It was another nightmare, wasn't it? Are you okay?"

"I'm fine. Sorry I woke you." Though Red couldn't see much in the dark room, she could hear her roomie turning over in bed. "Let's go back to sleep," Gretel said with a yawn.

"Okay," Red agreed. But just like the night before, it took her a while to fall asleep again. Now that she was awake, her brain just wouldn't turn off! Her mind kept replaying yesterday's embarrassing audition. And she was still worrying that she'd hurt Wolfgang's feelings when she turned down his offer to run lines with her. So it was no surprise that once she finally did doze off again, she overslept Saturday morning.

When she woke, Gretel was peacefully snoozing away. But Red was supposed to meet the other Grimm girls in a few minutes for today's treasure hunt!

Moving quietly so as not to disturb Gretel, who probably hadn't gotten enough rest either, Red dressed hurriedly in blue tights, a white tunic, and a blue-patterned skirt. After throwing on her red cloak, she grabbed a cookie from the common room to munch. Then she raced down five flights of stairs before pushing open the heavy wooden door that led across the castle drawbridge. Once she was outside, she ran around the side of Pink Castle to the Bouquet Garden, where Snow, Cinda, and Rapunzel were all waiting for her.

"Sorry I'm late," Red said breathlessly. A bouquet of deep red roses, white lilies, pink carnations, and green ferns growing on a nearby bush caught her eye and she stooped to inhale the bouquet's heavenly fragrance.

An extraordinary variety of flowers grew in the Bouquet Garden — roses, tulips, lilies, daisies, carnations, orchids, and dozens more. Unlike most flowers, the ones here actually bloomed together in attractive combinations all on one bush. So with a single flick of your wrist you could pick a beautifully arranged ready-made bouquet that contained many kinds of flowers!

"S'okay," Cinda told Red. "Rapunzel just got here, too."

"I had to, um, fix my hair," Rapunzel explained.

Which meant she'd cut it, of course. They could all see that it was way shorter than it had been last night, only reaching to the waist of the goth-style black gown she wore. However, as usual, not one of the three other Grimm girls commented on this. For some reason the fact that her hair grew an inch or so longer every hour was a touchy subject with Rapunzel. Since nobody wanted to risk offending her or making her uncomfortable, hair and fear of heights were topics they all avoided.

Just then, bonging sounds floated out of the windows of the Great Hall. The Hickory Dickory Dock clock was announcing that it was eleven o'clock.

"We'd better go," said Cinda.

Snow nodded anxiously. "Yeah. No telling how long this'll take, and we don't want to be caught in Neverwood Forest after the sun goes down." Her pale fingers toyed with the crystal amulet she wore on a silver chain around her neck. Inside the amulet was a four-leaf clover. She lowered her voice to a whisper. "It's haunted, you know."

Rapunzel rolled her eyes. "That's just superstition."

Red wished she hadn't said that. Snow was a big believer in superstition. Although she didn't yet have her real one-and-only charm like Cinda's slippers or Red's basket, Snow collected all kinds of good-luck charms, including her clover necklace.

Besides, in this case, Red feared Snow could be right. Even Gretel, who took more risks than she should out hiking around with her brother, Hansel, rarely ventured into Neverwood Forest. But Red kept her mouth shut. She didn't want to fuel Snow's nervousness.

"Fingers crossed we find the treasure," she said instead, as they trooped across the Academy grounds toward the forest.

"Yeah," said Cinda. "Just think what heroes we'd be."

"Can you imagine how excited Principal R would get if we brought him a pile of gold and jewels?" asked Snow.

"The Academy would be saved, which means he might even stop his alchemy experiments!" Red added.

"Too bad our school can't just sell off a couple of gold statues or tapestries or a few silver trays or something," Cinda put in. According to the Grimm Academy Handbook, the sale of Academy artifacts and property was strictly forbidden.

"About the treasure," Rapunzel said. "I hate to burst everyone's bubble, but maybe we should come up with a

Plan B? Just in case we don't find any after all? Or in case Grandmother Enchantress can't or won't help us? Or in case the treasure isn't what we hope it will be?"

She has a point, thought Red as they came to the edge of the forest. "If we need to, maybe we could *raise* money for the school," she suggested.

"By doing what?" asked Cinda. Without a moment's hesitation, she plunged ahead into the forest, leaving the other girls little choice but to follow.

"We could have a bake sale!" Red exclaimed. Then she glanced around. The trees grew so close together inside the forest that their branches blocked most of the sun, making it quite chilly. And a little creepy. She pulled her cape more tightly around her.

"I'm horrible at cooking," said Cinda. "How about a Sports Day competition instead? We could sell tickets to the villagers throughout Grimmlandia. They could come watch students compete." Cinda was great at sports, especially a game called masketball where players wore masks and shot balls at hoops on magical goals that moved around the court on their own.

Suddenly, Cinda halted. The path they were following had come to a *T*. "Hold on a minute. Where's the map?"

Snow had taken the mapestry last night to her room. She had a keen interest in embroidery and had wanted to study some of the stitches in the mapestry more closely so she could learn to copy them. Now she pulled the mapestry from the bag she carried and handed it over. Seeing it suddenly reminded Red of something.

"My basket! Oh, no, I meant to bring it!" Wolfgang had warned her to keep a close eye on it. And she'd intended to, especially since she feared he might try to steal it! But after oversleeping, she'd been in a hurry this morning and had accidentally gone off without it. "Maybe I should go back and get it."

"You can't go alone," Rapunzel insisted.

"Yeah, you'll get lost," said Snow.

"But if you really need it, we'll turn around," said Cinda.

"Well, I guess I don't really *need* it," Red said reluctantly. Boys weren't allowed in the girls' dorm and vice versa, so surely it would be safe in her room. "I do wish I had it, though."

Red did her best to forget about the basket as she and the other three girls huddled around the mapestry. Once more they studied the row of golden stitches on it that led halfway through the embroidered forest to the tiny embroidered cottage labeled with a big cross-stitch *X*. The cottage they all suspected must belong to Grandmother Enchantress. The place where they hoped to find the lost Treasure of Grimmlandia!

"Looks like we go right," said Cinda.

"Agreed," said Snow, and Rapunzel nodded.

"Okay," Red added, though she really had no clue if right was the *right* way to go. She was glad Cinda knew how to interpret the stitches. Because if Red was guiding them instead, they'd wind up lost for sure, map or no map. Besides having a crummy sense of direction, she also couldn't read a map to save her life!

"I thought of another way we could raise money if we don't find treasure," Rapunzel said as the girls started off again. "We could have a pet show with a pet talent contest and prizes."

Rapunzel was a real animal lover. She especially loved cats, and even kept some in her room in the dungeon. "We could charge everyone a fee for each pet they entered," she went on.

"If you entered all of your cats, you'd go bankrupt," Cinda teased her.

Rapunzel grinned. "True, but they're so beautiful and talented they'd win all the prizes." This made the others laugh.

"Or maybe we could set up a beauty salon," suggested Snow. "We could earn money cutting and styling hair."

"All good ideas, but they wouldn't really raise enough money to help the school, would they?" said Red. "Besides, nobody would want *me* to cut their hair," she added. "Last time I tried trimming my bangs I almost gave myself a bald patch!" The girls all laughed again at that.

As they continued along, the trees grew even thicker together. Very little light filtered through their branches so it was easy to stumble over the roots that snaked across the dirt path. The girls went single file with Red at the back of the line, no longer talking so they could concentrate on where they placed their feet.

Woot-woo! Woot-woo! a bird called out.

The mournful sound startled Red and made her heart pound. Seconds later, a low shadowy form ran in front of her. She gave a little yelp of surprise as it disappeared up a tree. "Was that a squirrel? It didn't quite look like one."

"I don't know. I'm getting scared," Snow replied. "We've never been this far into the forest before. It's really dark and spooky."

Red was glad she wasn't the only one who felt afraid. Mr. Hump-Dumpty was always warning them against venturing into this forest, and now his words kept running through her head. More bird sounds echoed from the trees. They seemed to say, *Keep owt! Keep owt!*

"Maybe we should all hold hands," Cinda called back. "So we won't get separated."

Was that the only reason Cinda was suggesting the idea? Red wondered. Or was she scared, too? At the front of the line, Cinda and Rapunzel caught hands.

Snow was ahead of her, so Red reached out to her. Instead of catching hold of Snow's fingers, though, she touched something hard and wooden. Red screamed and snatched back her hand. *"Aghhh!"* This made the other girls scream, too. They whirled around to look at her with big eyes.

"What's going on?" asked Cinda. "You scared us half to death!"

"I almost had a heart attack!" added Rapunzel.

"So did I," said Snow.

Red pointed to the ground by her feet. "Look! It's my basket!" she exclaimed. "It must have come all the way from my room on its own to find me!" The basket bounced and twirled around with excitement when it heard her voice. When she reached out, the basket hopped up as it had a moment ago, when she reached for Snow's hand. Its double handles slid over her arm so it could nestle close at her side.

As the girls grabbed hands and began to walk again, Rapunzel said to Red, "Remember a minute ago when you wished you had it?"

"Yeah," said Red.

"I wonder if it came to find you in answer to your wish," said Rapunzel.

Red considered that as she stepped over a fallen tree branch.

"Try wishing for something else," suggested Snow.

"Like what?" asked Red.

"Snacks!" Snow and Cinda said at the same time.

"Good idea," said Rapunzel. "I wish we'd thought to bring some. I'm starving."

"Me, too," said Red. That cookie she'd munched as she'd hurried down to the Bouquet Garden had been no substitute for breakfast. She dropped Snow's hand and paused in a small clearing where the ground was covered with lush green vines. "I wish you'd fill with snacks," she told the basket.

After she spoke, she raised the basket's lid to peek inside. The others stopped, waiting to see what would happen.

"It's empty. No snacks," she told them, shaking her head. Then she remembered the note that had been in the basket. Even though none of the rhymes they'd tried had worked, she decided to give it one more shot. There had been six blanks, so she would use six words to make her request.

"A tisket, a tasket. Please fill yourself with snacks, basket," she commanded. No sooner did the words leave her lips than her basket suddenly got a lot heavier. So heavy it pulled her arm downward.

"Whoa!" she exclaimed. She raised the lid again. "Hey, you guys, I think I just discovered one of the basket's powers!" She tilted it so they could see it was now filled with several kinds of fruit, nuts, and chips.

"Grimmtastic," said Snow. "I think that pretty much proves it. That basket has got to be your magical charm for sure!"

"No doubt about it," said Rapunzel, and Cinda nodded.

Red smiled, a warm, happy feeling filling her. For it seemed the basket really, truly must be her charm, since it had granted her wish. She set it on top of a tree stump with its lid open, and the girls took a snack break.

"Those grapes look yummy," said Rapunzel. She broke off a small bunch. "Look, I'm Ms. Jabberwocky." After tossing a grape up in the air, she caught it in her open mouth just the way the office assistant caught hot peppers. Everyone laughed.

"Ha! Good catch," said Cinda. As the girls gathered to stand around the stump, she took a banana.

"Mmm, that fruit looks so scrumptious," said Snow. "Too bad I'm allergic to it." She chose some walnuts instead.

"What happens if you eat fruit?" Cinda asked as she peeled an orange.

Snow made a face. "Depends. Some kinds give me an itchy, blotchy rash; others make me throw up. Blueberries make me feel sad and, well, blue. Bananas make me go bananas, as in, get all hyper. I haven't had a single bite of fruit since I was two years old and my dad figured out I was allergic. Sometimes I wonder if I even still am." She sighed, gazing longingly at the fruit in the basket. "But I'd better not risk it."

The girls were almost finished snacking when Red felt something tickle her ankle. She tried to wiggle her foot but couldn't. "Something's got hold of my ankle!" she exclaimed.

"Aghh! Mine, too!" cried Cinda.

"It's the vines! They're creeping around our feet, trying to wrap us up like mummies!" said Rapunzel. The girls began kicking and ripping at the vines. As soon as they managed to free themselves, Red snatched up her basket and they ran down the forest path to get away from the vicious vines.

Snap! Just as they finally slowed, Red heard a twig crack somewhere behind her. She heard the same sound a few seconds later. Was someone or some*thing* following them?

Snap! There it was a third time. "Did you hear that?" she called to Snow in a loud whisper.

"Hear what?"

"A snapping sound."

Halting, Snow dropped hold of Red's and Rapunzel's hands and cupped her own hands behind her ears. "I don't hear anything," she said after a few seconds.

"It stopped. Maybe I just imagined it," Red said doubtfully. "Maybe this creepy Neverwood Forest is turning me into a *basket* case."

"Hey, you two," Cinda yelled back to them. "Step it up!"

As Red and Snow hurried along the path, a loud, piercing howl came from somewhere close by. "Great grimmsters!" yelled Red, practically jumping out of her skin. On her arm, her basket gave a little jump, too.

"I w-wonder wh-what that was?" Snow's teeth were chattering.

"Sounded like a wolf," said Cinda when Red and Snow caught up to her.

Immediately, Red thought of Wolfgang. Were the rumors about him being able to shape-shift true? If she had to choose, she'd much rather *he* was out here roaming the forest than a real, wild wolf! Of course, he wasn't out here, though. Why would he be?

"I'm beginning to think we should've listened to Mr. Hump-Dumpty's warnings about this forest," said Rapunzel.

As her words died away, they heard another howl. The girls let out shrieks. They were so freaked out by now, they went running down the path.

"Ow!" A few seconds later, Red felt a sharp pebble in her ankle boot and had to stop.

"Wait up," she called. After setting her basket on the ground, she slipped off her boot and shook the pebble out. When she put it back on again, she looked around for the other girls. But they'd gone way ahead. They must not have heard her asking them to wait.

Snap! The sound sent Red scurrying down the path again after her friends. But after a dozen steps, she realized she'd left her basket sitting on the ground. She dashed back to get it. However, when she arrived at the spot where she thought her basket should have been, it wasn't there!

What if some forest creature had carried it off? Her heart pounded in her chest. She tried to calm down. More likely she'd simply gotten turned around somehow and this wasn't the place she'd left it after all. Typical! Her sense of direction was no sense at all.

"A tisket, a tasket. I wish you'd come back, basket!" she called out in a panic.

Thump! It worked! The basket landed at her feet.

Red snatched it up joyfully and hugged it to her. "I should have thought of that to begin with," she said as she slipped it onto her arm. "Instead of me trying to find you, from now on I'll get you to find *me*."

Standing in place, she turned in a complete circle, looking for her friends. She didn't see them. She didn't see the path, either. Everything looked the same on all sides of her. There were trees, vines, grass. But no path. *Argh.* She was lost!

7

Lost!

"Hey! I'm lost! Come find me!" Red shouted as she wandered through the forest. But none of her friends answered back. Probably too far away to hear her.

She looked down at her basket. "I don't suppose *you* could take me to my friends," she asked it hopefully. "Or bring them to me?"

Her basket wiggled side to side on her arm, like someone shaking their head no. Then it went still again.

"Is it because I'm too big to fit inside you?" she asked it.

The basket jiggled up and down on her arm.

"I'll take that as a yes," said Red. "So I guess you can only transport things that are smallish?"

The basket jiggled up and down again.

It's good to be learning more about how its powers work, thought Red. That knowledge might prove useful — *if* she ever got out of this grimmorrible forest again, that was!

She gazed up at the trees, hoping they might somehow give her a clue to her whereabouts. But they looked just like the trees everywhere else in the forest, except that here they seemed to grow even closer together. So close, in fact, that she couldn't even see where the sun was in the sky to figure out what time it was. It felt like they were purposely trying to turn day to night. *You're imagining things*, she scolded herself. Just like she'd imagined that someone was following her before.

Owooo! A piercing howl like the one they'd heard earlier prickled Red's skin. Only this time, it sounded much closer. There was a flapping of wings in the nearby trees. Startled birds flew up in the air.

Terrified, Red gritted her teeth, trying not to give in to panic. As a rule, wolves tried to avoid people, she remembered hearing once. Too late, she also remembered hearing that if you were ever lost in the woods, you should hug a tree and then stay put till someone found you.

But maybe it wasn't really too late to try the tree hugging thing. She looked around wildly for a suitable tree. One she could fit her arms around. After spotting a good prospect, she hooked the basket at her elbow and slid her arms around the tree.

There was a rustling sound. Then, to her surprise, the

tree's lower branches reached around her to hug her back! Well, this *was* Grimmlandia, after all. Enchantment came with the territory.

"Thanks," she told the tree. "I really needed a hug right now."

But then the hug began to get tighter. And tighter. "Stop it!" Red yelled, struggling. She slapped at the branches and managed to pull away, getting a scratch in the process.

She glared at the tree. "What is wrong with you, you dumb tree?"

Its branches gave a big shrug, as if to say, *What do you expect? This is Neverwood Forest — haven't you been warned?*

"Humpf! So much for hugging trees!" said Red. As she was rubbing her sore hand she heard a twig crunch again. *Snap!*

She whirled around so fast that her basket almost flew off her arm. "Cinda?" she called out hopefully. "Snow? Rapunzel?"

"Who walks these forests? If you are a friend in need of the sustenance that I can provide, make yourself known and I will help you," she called out when no one answered. It was a line from *Red Robin Hood*. It had just popped out of her mouth, and for some reason reciting it in a dramatic fashion helped calm her nerves.

To her surprise, she heard the sound of clapping. She looked at the hugging tree to see if it was clapping its branches. It wasn't.

"Bravo," a voice called out. "Well said, Vermillion."

Stumbling back in surprise, Red accidentally dropped her basket. Up ahead in the forest, Wolfgang stepped into view. "You!" She rushed forward, so glad help had arrived that she didn't even call him on using a red synonym instead of her name.

But then she remembered what she'd overheard him talking about with Ms. Wicked yesterday. Abruptly, she stopped a few feet from him, wondering what he was up to. "Uh, I mean, I was actually hoping you'd turn out to be my friends, but —"

"But I'll do in a pinch?" He looked around. Seeing only her, he said, "Are you lost out here?"

Her cheeks grew warm with embarrassment. "Yes. I mean no. I mean — well, *obviously*!"

They walked back to where her basket sat. Wolfgang eyed it curiously as it jumped up from the ground and slung itself over her arm again. Red hugged it protectively.

"So where are your friends?" he asked.

"If I knew that, I wouldn't exactly be lost, would I?" Back at school, she'd fudged the truth and told him she and her friends were going to pick flowers today. Had he guessed they'd come here? "I accidentally got separated from them while we were picking flowers," she said quickly. "What are you doing here anyway? Did you follow us?" That would explain the snapping sounds she'd heard. But what about the howling?

"Maybe." Wolfgang stopped at the hug-tree and leaned back against it. "Or maybe I just like forests."

Her basket swung on her arm as she lifted it to point at the tree. "Better watch it. That tree is weird."

He folded his arms over his chest, not looking worried in the least. "Yeah, I know. Everything in Neverwood has peculiarities of one kind or another."

Red raised her brows. What did that mean? Suddenly, this forest seemed that much more scary.

"Are your flowers in there?" he asked, nodding to her basket.

"Um, no. We didn't find any good ones," she fibbed quickly.

Wolfgang's eyebrows lifted. "Really? Maybe I can help. I know this part of the forest pretty well."

"Thanks, but I really need to catch up with my friends," said Red.

"Best thing to do is probably head back to the Academy. They'll eventually go there." He pushed off from the tree as if planning to lead her back to GA.

"No!" said Red. She didn't want to miss out on finding treasure, if that was to happen today. "Actually, we were all thinking of looking for the cottage where Grandmother Enchantress lives," she admitted. "Do you know where it is?"

A startled look crossed his face, but then he shrugged. "Sure. I know a shortcut. And there's a garden with a ton of flowers on the way. Come on." With that he took off. Not knowing what else to do, she followed.

After a dozen silent steps along the path, he spoke the lines that came after the ones she'd called out earlier. "It is I, Tiny John, an admirer of your kind deeds." After a dramatic pause, he went on. "Nay, more than a mere admirer, fair Red Robin Hood. And if you would permit me to join you in your lofty endeavor, you will find me an able companion and a most loyal friend." His voice was *sooo* magical. You couldn't help but pay attention when he was acting out a character!

"Hello?" Wolfgang shot her a glance, slowing to walk beside her as the path widened. "That's your cue to continue with the scene."

She sighed. "I already told you. I'm not going to audition, so there's no sense in practicing."

His hair ruffled a little, as if in annoyance. "You shouldn't give up just because of one bad experience," he counseled her. "You probably just need more practice. I'm up for helping, I mean, if you want."

"Thanks," she said, "but knowing my lines isn't the problem." She darted a sideways glance at him as they walked. "It's the stage fright. You said you get it, too. So how do you deal with it? Cinda suggested I picture the audience in their underwear, but . . ."

Grinning, Wolfgang flipped his brown hair out of his eyes. "That's crazy. Why would that work?"

Red laughed. "It doesn't! It only made me giggle to imagine Principal Ruh . . ." She stopped, her cheeks heating again. "Never mind. So what *does* work then?"

"Flowers," he announced.

"What?" she asked blankly.

He gestured at their surroundings.

Red glanced around and saw they were both standing knee-deep in a sea of colorful flowers! She'd been so interested in what he was saying that she hadn't noticed they'd reached a beautiful meadow full of daisies, cornflowers, and other blossoms she couldn't even name. The flowers didn't grow together as single bouquets like in the Bouquet Garden, but as separate, distinct plants.

Wolfgang bent and picked a handful of large, white daisies and vibrant blue cornflowers. "Open wide," he said, looking at her basket.

"Oh," she said, pulling up both sides of the hinged lid. She didn't really have time to waste picking flowers. Still, it was kind of sweet of him to pick them for her, and she did want to talk about acting for a few more minutes. Gazing up at him, she decided she really hoped she was wrong about him being part of E.V.I.L.

"So what does work?" she repeated. "To get rid of stage fright, I mean."

"Being prepared is number one. And you said you already know your lines. But beyond that there are other things you can try. Like taking a deep, calming breath before you begin your lines." He paused then, chuckling. "I remember once before a performance, I even wrote down all the things I was afraid might go wrong. And it helped!"

"You mean like that you might faint?" asked Red. She was following him around, holding her basket as he continued to pick and fill it with fragrant flowers.

"Right," he said. "Or get tongue-tied. Or that you'll start drooling or sneezing. Stuff like that."

"Hey, don't give me any ideas. I can think up enough things to worry about on my own," she said, and they both laughed.

"Sometimes just getting your fears down on paper seems to help stop them from happening. You sort of realize how silly they are." He stared into the distance as if thinking. "And I try to get inside my character's head until I'm almost part of him, instead of myself. Pretty soon, I'm ignoring the audience. It's like they aren't even there."

Red considered that for a minute. If she *was* going to audition again, which she wasn't, his ideas might be worth trying. Remembering that she was on a mission, she said, "So, I guess we'd better head for the cottage!"

Wolfgang nodded easily. "Sure. Follow me." Snatching her basket from her arms, he headed off, moving fast.

"Hey. Wait up!" she yelled after him. "Give me back my basket!"

For a moment Wolfgang hesitated up ahead on the path. He glanced over his shoulder at her and his gray eyes glinted in the dim light of the forest.

"Sorry," he said softly. "I can't." She thought she glimpsed an apologetic look on his face before he turned away.

Then suddenly he began to shape-shift. Red watched in shock as his ears grew large and pointy. His jacket changed to thick gray fur, and his hands and feet turned into paws. He sprouted a long gray tail. Dropping to all fours, he let out a piercing howl. With his jaws clamped around the basket handles, he bounded away!

8

Wolf

Red stared after Wolfgang, stunned. So he really could shape-shift! Which meant that it probably *had* been him howling before, scaring them all half to death for fun. Now it made sense why he hung out here — because wolves liked forests, right?

As the shock of seeing him shape-shift wore off, Red began to get mad! She took off down the path after him. When they were talking before, she'd *thought* they were becoming friends. She had even decided she might have misunderstood the conversation between Wolfgang and Ms. Wicked yesterday. But now he'd deserted her. And stolen her basket!

Remembering that she'd called her basket back to her earlier, she tried it again. "A tisket, a tasket. Come back to me, basket!" No luck. The basket didn't appear. Wait! She hadn't asked properly. She'd only filled in five of the six blanks. She tried again, her voice breathless from running. "A tisket, a tasket. Come back to me, *dear* basket," she called out. Still, nothing happened. *Weird*.

She could see Wolfgang running ahead, a gray speck in the distance. Maybe his teeth were hanging on to its handle too tightly for it to escape?

Now that he possessed it, was it possible the basket had become *his* magical charm? She didn't think magical charms could change who they belonged to, but she wasn't absolutely sure.

Owooo! She'd lost sight of him in the distance up ahead. Was he howling to help her follow him? Or maybe he couldn't help howling when he was in wolf form. Regardless, she headed in the direction of the sound. At least she hoped it was the right direction.

Luckily, because of recent rains and a slightly muddy path, Wolfgang's wolf paws had left tracks. She followed them, fearing she might be stuck in the forest forever if she lost him. He didn't seem to care that she might starve to death in this grimmideous forest before anyone could find her. *Thanks a lot, Wolfgang!*

This whole thing didn't make sense. He'd told her to guard her basket back in Scrying class. But that was before he'd talked to Ms. Wicked. Did she have some hold over him? Was that why he'd taken it? Or maybe that had been his plan all along. Had his kindness merely been a trick? Was he a member of E.V.I.L. after all?

A lump of anger formed in Red's throat. This wasn't fair! *No, it isn't,* said a little voice inside her head. *So what are you going to do about it?*

"I'm not going to let him get away with it, that's what!" Red replied out loud.

The tracks led straight to a small stone cottage at the heart of the wood. *Perfect!* Red bounced on her toes with glee when she saw it. This must be the cottage of Grandmother Enchantress! She was disappointed to see no sign of her friends. Maybe they were inside. Maybe Wolfgang was, too. Determined to confront him and to get back her basket, Red knocked on the door.

"Come in!" called a low, croaky voice.

The room Red entered was bright and cheery. Shelves of books lined the walls, plants in pots hung here and there, and a colorful hooked rug lay on the floor. But there was no Wolfgang.

An ancient woman was sitting in an old oak rocking chair that was creaking back and forth. Her hair was rather short and gray under her kerchief, and she wore knitted gloves and spectacles. She was wrapped in a colorful patchwork quilt up to her chin.

"Are you Grandmother Enchantress?" Red asked.

The woman nodded.

Thrilled to meet such a legend, Red curtsied. "I'm Red Riding Hood."

"Don't come too close," the enchantress warned in a low, growly voice. "I've got a cold."

"Oh! I'm sorry," said Red. Then she added politely, "Can I make you a cup of hot tea? Or bake you some cookies?"

"No, dearie, just have a seat so we can chat, will you?"

Gingerly, Red sat on the cozy flowered couch across from the enchantress. For being so old and sick, she was a surprisingly energetic rocker. Red hoped the ancient woman's chair wouldn't tip over backward.

"I wonder if you could help me," Red began. "I'm looking for a boy named Wolfgang and some friends of mi —"

"Ah, Wolfgang. Such a nice boy," interrupted the enchantress. "Don't you think so?"

Red frowned. "Well, I *did*," she said. "Until he stole something of mine."

Grandmother Enchantress lifted a dark eyebrow. "That doesn't sound like the Wolfgang I know. Perhaps he only *borrowed* your basket."

"*Huh?* How did you know it was a basket? I didn't tell you." Red sat forward eagerly. "Did he come here before me?" she asked, her eyes searching the cottage.

93

Grandmother Enchantress's chair paused a few beats before resuming its rocking. "He did," she said, "but he's long gone now. I wouldn't waste any more time trying to find him if I were you. Better just go on back to the Academy."

Back to the Academy? How did she know that was where Red had come from? And it almost sounded like the enchantress was trying to get rid of her!

"Actually," said Red, "I'm not that great with directions. Is it okay if I wait here for my friends? I got separated from them, you see. We were trying to find your cottage because —" She paused, unsure whether or not she should say anything more.

But legend had it that the enchantress was a good person. Someone who was utterly trustworthy. So she couldn't possibly be associated with E.V.I.L.!

Quickly, Red explained all about the mapestry, and the treasure she and her friends were hoping to find.

"And you thought you'd find the treasure here?" the enchantress asked. "What did you think it would be?" She'd stopped rocking. Her gloved hands gripped the arms of her chair.

"Since the mapestry was leading us to your cottage, we were kind of hoping *you* would know," said Red.

"I see." The enchantress began rocking again. "I'm afraid I know nothing about any treasure," she said. Her voice sounded much stronger now than it had at the beginning of their visit. "The mapestry, as you call it, is undoubtedly a hoax."

"Oh," Red said, feeling terribly let down.

"I think it would be best for you and your friends to forget about hunting for treasure. Concentrate on your studies instead."

Though her heart felt heavy with disappointment, Red managed to say, "Thank you for the advice." As the wisest person in Grimmlandia, Grandmother Enchantress must know what she was talking about.

Changing the subject, the enchantress said, "So, Wolfgang tells me you want to act. He says there's a part in a play at the Academy that you're just right for."

"Um, I'm not sure about that," Red replied. She was surprised that Wolfgang had talked about her to the enchantress. At the same time, she felt pleased that he thought she was "just right" for the part of Red Robin Hood.

Grandmother Enchantress pulled her kerchief lower around her face and smiled at her. "That Wolfgang has a good head on his shoulders. You should listen to him."

"Uh. Okay," Red said. This legendary lady obviously thought highly of Wolfgang. So maybe he wasn't all bad. She remembered how apologetic he'd looked just before he'd changed into a wolf and run off. Maybe she'd been right to think that Ms. Wicked had some hold over him. After class, it *had* kind of sounded like she'd *ordered* him to steal her basket. But he wouldn't really turn it over to Ms. Wicked, would he?

The enchantress had begun to rock more energetically again. Her eyes were twinkling. They were gray, Red noticed. Just like Wolfgang's.

"My, what nice gray eyes you have!" she blurted. Then immediately she worried that she was being rude for saying something so personal.

But the enchantress didn't seem to mind. "Why, thank you," she said, batting her eyelashes in a teasing way. "All the better to see you with." Then she leaned forward in her chair. "Forgive the nosy question, but I'm wondering if there's a special boy you like at school?"

Red looked down, feeling her cheeks flush. Because for some reason a picture of Wolfgang leaped into her head. "I . . . uh . . . not really," she mumbled. Had she thought of him just because they'd been talking about him? Or *did* she like him?

As the enchantress rambled on about what a wonderful boy Wolfgang was, but so underappreciated by other students, Red suddenly noticed the woman's feet. She was wearing sneakers, which stuck out from under the bottom edge of the patchwork quilt!

"My, what big feet you have!" Red blurted in surprise. Then she clapped a hand over her mouth, totally embarrassed. What was wrong with her? She knew better than to comment on the size of people's feet!

However, Grandmother Enchantress only laughed. "All the better to get around the forest with," she said.

"Oh, uh-huh," said Red. She was beginning to think that there was something kind of fishy about the enchantress. Only she couldn't quite put her finger on what it was.

Then she noticed something long and shadowy sticking out the back of the rocking chair. The long, shadowy thing was switching back and forth like the Hickory Dickory Dock clock pendulum.

It was a *tail*, she suddenly realized. A *wolf's* tail, to be exact. Wolfgang! Her eyes narrowed. Though he'd somehow managed to disguise himself as Grandmother Enchantress, it was definitely him. And for some reason he was starting to shift into a wolf again — at least his tail was.

Seemingly oblivious to what was happening, the phony enchantress went on praising Wolfgang's many admirable qualities, including (according to her — er, *him*) his sensitivity to others, his love of nature, and his intelligence.

"Yeah, but no one is perfect. He must have *some* faults," Red insisted. Casually, her eyes roved the room, searching for her basket. Wolfgang had to have hidden it somewhere!

The wolf-enchantress blinked. "Um. Yes. Of course he does," she said. "Though I can't think of any. I'm sure they're small faults. Hardly worth mentioning."

Out of the corner of her eye Red caught a small movement near the floor, under a cloth lying between the rocking chair and the couch. *Aha*, she thought. *So that's where Wolfgang (aka Grandmother Enchantress) hid it.* He must have cast some kind of spell on the basket to keep it still, or else it surely would have leaped into her lap as soon as she'd arrived.

"What an interesting basket you have," Red couldn't resist saying as she jumped from the couch. In two quick steps she was reaching under the cloth and grabbing the basket. "Only it's not yours. Is it . . . Wolfgang?"

Knock! Knock! Red's gaze flew to the cottage door. She heard her friends talking outside.

Startled, the fake enchantress sprang from the rocking chair with a liveliness you'd expect from someone a quarter of the real Grandmother Enchantress's age. Maybe even younger. Say the age of a thirteen-year-old boy, er, *wolf*?

As Red clutched her basket firmly in her arms, Wolfgang threw off the kerchief and spectacles and grinned somewhat wolfishly. "You got me, Cerise."

"My name's Red, you . . . basket-napper!" she yelled.

"Yeah, about that." His eyes went to her basket.

She swung it behind her back, holding its handles tight with both hands. Perhaps because of the fierce look she sent him, or maybe because he knew her friends were right outside the door, Wolfgang didn't even *try* to take it from her. Instead, he tossed off the rest of his disguise, leaped out a window at the side of the cottage, and landed outside. There, he fully shape-shifted into wolf form, and ran off. *Owooo!*

Together Again

$\mathcal{S}$till clutching her basket, Red ran to open the door. Her friends' faces lit up with surprised pleasure when they saw her.

"I'm so glad you're here!" Snow exclaimed. She wrapped both arms around Red. Rapunzel and Cinda joined in, making it a four-way hug.

"We were so worried about you!" said Cinda when they finally let go. She peered around Red into the cottage. "Is Grandmother Enchantress here?"

"No, but wait till I tell you —" But before Red could tell them about Wolfgang and everything, Rapunzel interrupted. "When we realized you weren't behind us, we tried to find you."

Snow nodded. "We called out over and over, but you didn't answer."

In a rush, Red explained how she'd gotten separated

from them. "I tried to find you, too, but I only got more and more lost."

"We hoped you'd somehow find your way here to the cottage," Cinda said. "We would've been here sooner ourselves if we hadn't lost the mapestry."

"Oh, no!" Red said. Drawing her friends inside, she shut the door behind them. "Where? How did it happen?"

Cinda looked a bit shame-faced. "I had folded it and stuck it in my pocket. It didn't really fit all that well, so it must have fallen out without my realizing it. I'm so sorry!"

Losing the mapestry was actually a gigantic disappointment, but Red gave Cinda's hand a quick, gentle squeeze. "Could've happened to anyone," she assured her. "Especially me. I'm pretty much the queen of anything to do with the word *lost*!"

"We retraced our steps as best we could, but no luck," said Snow. "It's like it just disappeared. Poof!"

Putting aside the subject of the mapestry for now, Red began to recount some of what had happened since they'd lost each other. "Wolfgang found me. And you know those rumors about him being able to shape-shift? Well, they're not just rumors." She paused to let that sink in. "It was him making those wolf howls we heard earlier. He was following us, and he led me here."

"Why?" asked Snow.

"I don't know exactly. If you'd come two seconds sooner, you could have asked him yourself." She pointed to the window. "He took off through there after you knocked."

"Hmm. I'm worried about the enchantress. I mean, where is she? What if she's in trouble?" said Cinda.

"How about if we do a little snooping?" suggested Rapunzel, gazing around the cottage. "To see if she left a note or some clue to her whereabouts."

"Yeah, maybe we'll turn up some clues to the treasure while we're at it," said Snow.

"It was my fault Wolfgang followed us," Red admitted as she and her friends began to poke around. "I told him we were all going flower picking today, and —"

"Flower picking?" Cinda quickly closed a cupboard door on a magical sugar bowl that had tried to hop out as soon as she'd opened it.

"I had to tell him *something*," said Red. "But I never told him we were going to Neverwood Forest. You see, he —"

"So he must have figured it out on his own," Cinda interrupted again. She glanced over her shoulder at Red. "You didn't tell him about the treasure though, right?"

"Not exactly," Red hedged. After all, she thought she'd been talking to Grandmother Enchantress when she'd revealed stuff about the mapestry and the treasure! She knew she should tell the rest of the truth, but first she needed to explain a few other things.

She set her basket on the kitchen table. "Just now, after he found me in the forest, he stole my basket, and then pretended to be the enchantress," she said. Going over to the hooked rug, she pulled up the edge of it and peeked under. She didn't see anything suspicious like a trapdoor or a loose floorboard where treasure might be hidden, however.

"He did what?" Rapunzel exclaimed just as she lifted the lid from a candy dish. She set it down again fast when the tiny seedlike firecracker candies inside began to explode like popped corn. She, Snow, and Cinda exchanged concerned looks.

Going back to the very beginning, Red explained about Wolfgang offering to help her run lines after school was out.

"Ha! I always thought he liked you," interrupted Snow as she gently untangled a flower blossom from her hair. It had snaked down from one of the hanging pots and tucked itself behind her ear while she was poking through the nooks and crannies of a rolltop desk in one corner of the cottage.

Cinda nodded, pushing her long yellow hair back over one shoulder as she scanned the books on the enchantress's bookshelves. "Yeah, I noticed him staring at you at lunch on my first day at the Academy."

"What? No." Once more Red could feel her cheeks warming. Turning away, she studied a portrait of a young woman on the wall beside the door. It was probably the enchantress herself. From a long time ago. Odd how the eyes seemed to look right into hers . . . and kind of follow her. "He just wanted to talk more about the auditions," she added.

"Uh-huh," said Rapunzel. She grinned, showing she didn't believe that for a minute. "Because as everyone knows, he's such a *social* guy," she joked. "So friendly and outgoing."

"He's not *usually* social," Cinda said to Rapunzel, "but he *is* suddenly buddying up with the oddest people. Don't forget that we all saw him chatting it up with my stepsisters at lunch yesterday."

And he'd been chatting with Ms. Wicked, too, of course. Red moved away from the portrait and opened a closet. Immediately, the mop inside began to dance around and a bottle of liquid soap started blowing out bubbles. *Snick!* She shut the door again before they could escape.

"He's up to *something*. That's for sure," said Rapunzel.

Red leaned against the closet door. "There's more I didn't tell you," she said slowly.

"What?" Cinda asked, abandoning the bookshelves.

"Yesterday I heard Ms. Wicked and Wolfgang talking," Red admitted. "And I think Ms. Wicked *told* Wolfgang to steal my basket from me."

"*What?*" Snow said, going pale. "I'm so sorry!"

"It's not your fault," Red told her. "But I should tell you that she also mentioned the Society. So she definitely knows about it."

At this, Snow went even paler. "Is she a member?"

"And is Wolfgang a member of the Society, too?" Cinda asked. "Is that why he did what Ms. Wicked asked and tried to steal your basket?"

"I hope not. I don't know." Red went over to the table and gave her basket a fond pat, saying, "All I know is I'm glad I got my basket back."

As they continued their searching, she outlined all that had happened up till the time they'd arrived at the cottage. She explained how she'd guessed Wolfgang had disguised himself as the enchantress when she spotted the shadowy tail twitching back and forth. "Plus, he kept telling me stuff I didn't think the real Grandmother Enchantress would say."

Rapunzel cocked her head. "Like what?"

Red squirmed a little under her gaze. "Like she — I mean, *he* — kept going on about what a great guy Wolfgang was."

Cinda peeked under the rocking chair's cushion, then plopped down to sit. "Sounds like he was trying to get you to trust him."

"But why?" asked Red. She hung up a sparkly white robe that had fallen off a coatrack while she was checking its pockets. There'd been nothing in them, of course. Zippo. Nada.

"Hello?" said Rapunzel. "So you wouldn't suspect him of belonging to E.V.I.L.? And so you'd tell him more stuff about what we're doing?"

"Um, yeah, about that," Red said slowly. "When I thought he was the enchantress, the stuff about the mapestry and treasure kind of . . . slipped out."

The other girls all gasped. But then Cinda said kindly, "Could have happened to any one of us, Red. He tricked you into it."

"You do know now that you absolutely cannot trust him, right?" Snow told Red. "No more than we can trust my stepmom."

"Yeah, I guess," Red said ruefully. Wolfgang was *shifty*, and not just when it came to his shape-shifting abilities! Her friends must be right about him. She felt a little let down about what Cinda and Rapunzel had said, though. She'd thought maybe Wolfgang had talked himself up to impress her. She'd thought he really did like her and had been hoping she might like him back. After all, why ask if there was a special boy she liked at school if he wasn't hoping she'd name *him*?

Red glanced over at a window — the one Wolfgang had departed through. The shadows had grown deep. It was later than she'd realized.

"We'd better go," she said, picking up her basket. "It'll be dark soon!"

10

The Enchantress

With Cinda in the lead, the girls left the cottage and started back through the forest toward the Academy. They were all wishing they'd met the real Grandmother Enchantress and were more than a little disappointed they hadn't found treasure, either.

"Can you guys get us out of here? Even without the mapestry?" Red asked the others.

"I think so," Cinda said. "I memorized most of it." She looked at Snow and Rapunzel, a question in her eyes.

"I remember it, sort of," said Snow.

"Me, too," said Rapunzel.

The woods grew darker and darker as they walked. Several times, they reached a point where they were unsure of their directions. Red felt bad that she had no clue which way to go and could only wait as the other three girls tried to figure it out.

"Too bad we don't have a lantern," said Cinda.

"Yeah," said Red.

"Could your basket bring us one?" asked Snow.

"Duh," Red said, tapping the palm of her hand against the side of her head. "*I* should have thought of that." She looked down at her basket. "A tisket, a tasket. Please bring us a lantern, basket," she said. Within seconds her basket grew heavier.

"Whoops!" The unexpected weight made her arm drop.

After setting the basket on the ground, Red opened its lid. A small lantern lay on top of the flowers she and Wolfgang had picked a couple of hours ago.

"Voilà!" With a theatrical flourish she pulled out the lantern. "For you, mademoiselle," she said, handing it to Cinda, who grinned and curtsied in return.

"We'll need matches, too," Rapunzel noted.

After shutting the basket's lid, Red made the request. When she reopened the basket, a few wooden matches were lying atop the flowers.

As the other girls tried to get the lantern to light, Red suddenly got a brilliant idea. Quickly, she made a third request of the basket. And when she opened its lid, her wish had come true. She pulled out the object she'd asked for and handed it to Cinda.

"The mapestry!" Cinda exclaimed. Just then, the lantern flared to life revealing a smudge of dried mud on one edge of the map. The smudge was in the shape of a paw print! A few strands of gray fur the exact color of a wolf's coat were caught in it.

"Wolfgang must have found the mapestry on his way back to the Academy!" said Cinda. She scratched at the dried mud with her fingernail, easily brushing it away.

A satisfied smile flashed across Rapunzel's face. "Won't he be surprised when he discovers he no longer has it."

"Too bad he knows it's a treasure map since I blabbed about it when I thought he was the enchantress," Red said with a frown. What if he told E.V.I.L. about the mapestry? She was just shutting the basket again when the lantern light glinted off something shiny hidden among the flowers.

"Hey! There's something else in here, too," she said. She dug under the flowers and lifted out a round glass object about the size of a large grapefruit.

"It's a crystal ball!" she said, holding it up so the others could see. She was surprised at how light it was. It weighed no more than a feather! If it had been one of the clunky, heavy crystal balls from Scrying class instead, she surely would have noticed the extra weight in her basket before now.

The girls all gathered around to study the ball. "Where do you think it came from?" Snow asked.

"From Grandmother Enchantress's cottage?" Red guessed, turning the ball over and over in her hands.

"Wolfgang must have put it in there. Maybe he stole it from her, like he tried to steal your basket," said Cinda.

"How would he know it was there, though?" asked Red. She passed the ball to Rapunzel, who studied it for a few seconds, then gave it to Cinda.

"He could have accidentally found it," Rapunzel suggested. She threaded her fingers through her long dark hair and began re-braiding it. It looked as if it had already grown several inches since she'd cut it that afternoon. "Or maybe he spied on Grandmother Enchantress. He does hang out in the woods a lot."

"If this ball really does belong to the enchantress, wouldn't she have put some kind of magical spell on it to protect it against being stolen?" Snow asked, leaning over to study it with Cinda.

"Hmm. Good question," said Red. She also wondered why Ms. Wicked had wanted Wolfgang to steal her basket at all, unless she thought he could make its magic work for him. It was Red's magical charm. Didn't they know that meant its magic would work for her alone? Only how did the ball come to be in the basket if she was the only one who could make the basket work? It was all so confusing.

Woot-owt! Woot-owt! Suddenly, great big pairs of owl eyes peered at them from high in the darkness on all sides. They were surrounded!

"Let's get going," said Snow, looking creeped out.

"Yeah," said Red, more than a little weirded out herself. She picked up her basket and set the crystal ball back inside it.

She was about to close its lid when, much to the girls' surprise, a sparkly pink mist began to swirl inside the ball. From out of the mist appeared an ancient, lined face. When it actually spoke, all four girls gasped.

Red was so startled that she dropped her basket! Its lid snapped shut. "Oops! Sorry!" She bent and quickly pushed the lid open again, and the girls all stared down at the face in the crystal ball.

"Greetings, Grimm girls, I'm Grandmother Enchantress," said the face. Her voice had a mystical, magical quality, and her intelligent gray eyes seemed to be studying them as hard as they were studying her. However, unlike the girls, she seemed unsurprised to see them. "I take it you have my crystal ball," she said. Then she laughed. "Well, of course you do. Or I wouldn't be speaking to you."

For a moment none of the girls spoke. Then they all curtseyed to the enchantress at once. Despite her friendly tone they were completely in awe of her!

Finally, Red found her tongue. "Pleased to meet you, Grandmother Enchantress. I'm Red. Red Riding Hood, that is. And these are my friends, Cinda, Snow, and Rapunzel." She pointed to each in turn. "We're all in school together at Grimm Academy, and —" Worried that the enchantress might think they'd stolen her crystal ball, Red rushed to explain that they'd actually found it by accident.

But before she could utter another word, the enchantress interrupted. "There's no time to lose, little Grimmlins," she told them, peering up at the trees. "I can see that you're in the forest and that the sky is dark. Neverwood becomes more dangerous at night. You must hurry! Wait! I'll pop out of this ball and help you find your way back to the Academy."

With that, the sparkly pink mist began to swirl inside the ball again, obscuring Grandmother Enchantress's face. Then suddenly the mist was *outside* the ball and growing larger. All at once the mist vanished, and in its place stood the actual enchantress! Dressed in a long, flowing gown and cloak, she was taller than Red had expected, and quite thin, too. But then it was hard to gauge someone's height when all you could see of them was a head inside a ball!

"Brr," the enchantress said. "It's cold out here in the real world." She pulled the hood of her purple cloak over her hair and whipped the body of it more closely around herself. "It was much warmer inside my ball."

"You mean you were actually *inside* it?" Red asked as she picked up her basket again. "Not just looking through it from somewhere else?"

"I can do both," the enchantress informed them casually as if such amazing magical power was easy for her. "Now let's get moving. Before we all catch our death of cold. Or meet some unpleasant fate out here."

Following the enchantress's lead, the Grimm girls scurried through the forest, with Cinda holding the lantern. Instead of walking single file, they all bunched up as much as they could, trying to stay warm. Despite her advanced years, the enchantress had no trouble keeping up. In fact, the girls had to quicken their pace a little to keep up with *her*!

When they came to a branch blocking their path, Rapunzel held it back so that the others could pass. The branch tried to curl around Rapunzel's arm.

"Careful. Watch the trees around here," Grandmother Enchantress warned, batting the groping branch back with a bony hand. "They can be a bit clingy."

"I know," said Red. "When I was lost earlier, one of them tried to give me the hug of death!"

Snow and the other girls gasped and glanced warily at the surrounding trees. "Well, maybe I'm being a little overly dramatic," Red admitted. "But it did almost squeeze the breath out of me."

"Hurry! We go left here. Then right," said the enchantress, calling out turns as they came to forks in the path. When she wasn't giving directions, she was asking questions.

The girls took turns explaining about Red's basket, and how they'd become certain it must be her magic charm. And about the grand ball they'd attended at the Academy not long ago, and how Cinda's magic charm slippers had helped them discover the mapestry under a loose stone floor tile in the Great Hall. And lastly, about the pumpkin they'd watched disappear off the edge of the mapestry.

"Magical charms only come to those of good heart," Grandmother Enchantress commented in a wise tone. "And, yes, I know all about the mapestry. I helped Jacob and Wilhelm Grimm hide it in the Hall many, many years ago."

"You did?" said Red, ducking under some low-hanging vines. "Why?" Thinking about what else the enchantress had said, Red was pleased to think that she and Cinda had been judged to have good hearts. But Snow and Rapunzel also had good hearts. She hoped their charms would appear soon, too.

"Why?" repeated the enchantress. "To keep it from falling into the wrong hands, of course. Why else does one hide things?" She smiled at Red and the smile made her look *years* younger. Not a day over a hundred, anyway.

Then suddenly her smile faded. "We're almost back to the Academy. There's not much time, so listen well to what I'm going to say. Your ability to discover the mapestry means that the spell I put on it long ago — at Jacob and Wilhelm's urging — has been critically weakened. And that can only mean that a certain dark force is at work again."

"E.V.I.L.," Red said quickly.

"We know they've started up again," added Rapunzel. "In fact, we think Wolf —"

But before she could finish saying that the girls suspected Wolfgang of being a member of E.V.I.L., the enchantress said, "I know you suspect him. I saw and heard everything back at the cottage."

"Huh? How? We didn't see you!" said Cinda, sounding as embarrassed as Red felt to realize that the enchantress must have seen them snooping.

Red thought for a moment. "The portrait on the wall!" she exclaimed. "When I looked at it, your eyes stared straight into mine. You watched us through it!"

The enchantress didn't deny it, which meant Red had guessed right. But if the enchantress had been gazing through the portrait *before* Red's friends arrived, it meant she'd watched and heard the conversation between Wolfgang and her, too. *Double embarrassing!*

"The Exceptional Villains In Literature Society is villainous indeed," Grandmother Enchantress told them. "But someone outside the walls of Neverwood must be pulling their strings. The protective spells that keep Grimmlandia safe from the outside world can only be weakened if magic from Grimmlandia is being spirited *out*. E.V.I.L. is getting help from someone or something beyond the wall that surrounds the realm. Unfortunately, we don't yet know who or what is helping them."

What does she mean by "we"? wondered Red. She had a million more questions besides that one, but by now they'd reached the edge of the forest. The Academy loomed up ahead of them. "What will happen if the protective spells around Grimmlandia grow *too* weak?" Red asked.

The ancient woman's face twisted with a bleak expression. "It would mean the end of Grimmlandia," she said in a voice full of dread. "We'd be swallowed up into the Nothingterror."

The Grimm girls gasped in horror.

"Many of us are working to make sure that never happens," the enchantress reassured them. "And you can help, too."

"How?" asked Rapunzel. They'd drawn even with the Bouquet Garden and were approaching the drawbridge to Pink Castle now.

But the enchantress didn't reply. As she stared toward the Academy, something caught her attention and her eyes narrowed with dislike. "I must go now," she said hastily. "Talk to Wolfgang. See my crystal ball safely into his hands. It's important."

Before Red could protest that Wolfgang was exactly the *wrong* person to entrust the enchantress's crystal ball to, the pink mist materialized again. It quickly engulfed the enchantress and then moved to hover over Red's basket. As Red opened the lid, the mist streamed into the ball as if being sucked through a straw.

"Hide the mapestry. Guard it well," said the enchantress's voice, sounding far away now. Seconds later the mist evaporated and the ball was transparent again.

"Why do you think she left in such a hurry?" Snow asked worriedly as they crossed the drawbridge.

"Maybe there's something or someone here she wants to avoid," said Red.

"Or some*ones*," said Rapunzel. "Like members of E.V.I.L.!"

Exactly, thought Red. She wished the enchantress had said who was working with her to make sure Grimmlandia never got swallowed up by the Dark Nothingterror. The girls should have asked! Then they'd have known for sure who they could trust.

Gazing warily at the Academy, she slipped the mapestry into her basket. Good thing, too. Because no sooner were they through the drawbridge door than Ms. Wicked appeared. *Had the enchantress somehow sensed that she'd been lurking here?* Red wondered.

Her basket wriggled from her wrist to her elbow and hugged her side more closely as the teacher glanced its way. But then Ms. Wicked's eyes went to Cinda's lantern and from there to Snow. "Your hair is a tangled mess!" she snapped at her stepdaughter. "What have you and your little friends been doing out so late?"

Snow's pale face flushed rosy pink. "I-I — we . . ." she mumbled. Actually, Red thought Snow's hair looked kind of cute, all tousled and a bit wavy from the night air. But Snow had never been able to stand up to her stepmom. It must be mortifying to her that Ms. Wicked was so openly mean to her. Not to mention that she was likely a part of E.V.I.L., too!

"My fault," Red blurted. "I went for a walk to pick flowers and got lost. Snow, Cinda, and Rapunzel found me."

"And now we're starving!" added Cinda.

"Yeah! See you, Ms. Wicked," said Rapunzel.

"Last one to reach the dorm is a rotten goose egg!" Red said cheerfully. She grabbed one of Snow's hands and Rapunzel grabbed the other. With Cinda close on their heels, they rushed Snow off to the grand staircase just beyond the entrance before Ms. Wicked could say anything else mean to her.

Or ask the girls another question they wouldn't want to answer.

11

The Note

"Slow down," yelled Rapunzel as they left the grand staircase and started up the twisty stairs that led from the fourth floor up to the dorm towers. Just making it this far was a challenge for her since she rarely ventured beyond the third floor.

Red looked back and saw that Rapunzel's knuckles were white as she clung to the railing. She was truly terrified of going any higher.

"Sorry!" said Red. Handing her basket to Snow, she dropped back and took Rapunzel's arm. Cinda and Snow moved two steps below them, so that Rapunzel could set the pace for all four girls.

"Take deep breaths," coached Cinda.

"And think happy thoughts," added Snow.

"Uh-huh," said Rapunzel, her voice thready and frail with fear.

With one arm around Red and one hand on the railing, Rapunzel slowly climbed the stairs upward. Once Rapunzel was inside the dorm she'd be fine, Red knew, as long as she stayed away from windows and avoided the outside walkways.

After the girls reached the sixth-floor dorm in Pearl Tower, they crossed to the alcove Red shared with Gretel. On the way past one of the common-room tables, Red reached into the cookie jar on top. It was empty! Cleaned out by that cookie-scarfing Gretel, no doubt. Luckily, Red had anticipated such a possibility and hidden some cookies away in her room. If she was starving, the other girls must be, too. Dinner wasn't served in the Great Hall until six thirty and that was still an hour away!

"Just a second," said Snow. She darted into her room for something, and when she came out, Red saw that she held her hairbrush and was running it through her hair. Poor Snow! As usual, Ms. Wicked's criticism must have struck a nerve. How awful to have a stepmom that was so mean!

Without saying why, Red gave the poor girl a quick hug. Snow sent her a sweet smile in return. As the four Grimm girls entered Red's room, a bluebird flitted in from the window. It zoomed straight to Red and perched on her shoulder. It was holding a note! The written kind, but of course it was tweeting the musical kind as well. When she took the folded note, the bird flitted away again.

While Red opened the note, Snow took the basket and set it on her desk. "It's from Wolfgang," Red said in surprise. After silently scanning it first, she read it aloud. "'Meet me at the library tonight at eight. Urgent. Signed, Wolfgang.'"

"He has a lot of nerve!" huffed Rapunzel. "Asking you to meet up after he stole your stuff and tricked you by pretending to be the enchantress?"

"Shh!" said Cinda peeking outside the curtain to check for eavesdroppers. "Okay, the coast is clear." And luckily, Gretel wasn't in, so the girls could talk in private.

It was nice to hear Rapunzel being indignant on her behalf, thought Red. Her feistiness must mean she'd already recovered from her trip upstairs! Nevertheless, the girls still sat on the rug so that Rapunzel wouldn't have to climb the ladder to sit on Red's tall bed.

Jumping up again, Red raided the cookie stash in her desk. "Fear not the pangs of hunger," she intoned dramatically as she handed them around. "Think you that Red Robin Hood would stand by and see you starve?" She spread her arms wide. "Verily I say to you I would not!"

Her friends giggled. However, despite her dramatic mini-performance, no one mentioned the upcoming audition on

Monday or urged her to reconsider trying out. It sort of hurt her feelings, actually. They knew that acting in a play had always been her big dream. Was it possible that after her failure on Friday they now doubted her talent?

"I'm *sooo* exhausted," Snow announced. After tossing her brush aside, she took a big bite of cookie.

"Me, too!" said Rapunzel.

"Me, three," added Cinda. She flopped back on her elbows and stretched her legs out in front of her. As she munched her cookie, she looked up at Red. "So are you going to meet him?" she asked, returning to the subject of Wolfgang's note.

"Guess I'd better," Red replied, nibbling her cookie. "I have to give him the enchantress's ball, remember?" She didn't want to hand it over, though. It seemed like a big mistake to trust him with it.

"Maybe we'd better come with you," said Rapunzel. She'd scooted to sit cross-legged behind Cinda and was busily braiding Cinda's hair.

"Won't that make him feel like he's being ganged up on?" asked Snow before Red could reply.

Rapunzel frowned as she wove Cinda's hair. "Who cares? Maybe he deserves it."

"Grandmother Enchantress must trust Wolfgang though," Cinda mused. "Otherwise she wouldn't have asked us to give him her ball. So maybe we're wrong about him being a member of the Society." She looked over at Red. "Even if he did try to take your basket. And even if you did hear him talking to Ms. Wicked. There could be something else going on that we don't know about. You could at least ask him."

"*Humpf,*" said Rapunzel. "Maybe. But first he's got some grimmajor explaining to do."

"Definitely," said Snow. Getting up from the rug, she went to Red's desk and fetched the basket. "I want to see if the mapestry's changed," she told the others. But when she tried to open the lid of the basket it stayed firmly closed, just like it had for Gretel.

"I think it only opens for me," said Red.

"Ah." Snow passed her the basket. "Like how only Cinda can wear her glass slippers. It's a magical charm thing. I get it."

Rapunzel glanced over at Red. "If you're the only one who can open your basket, how did the crystal ball get in there?"

Red had been wondering about that, too, of course. She thought harder about it as she opened the basket and pulled out the mapestry. Suddenly, an explanation came to her. "I left the lid open while Wolfgang and I were picking flowers. It was still open when he stole my basket. He must have found the ball and put it inside before shutting the lid!"

Appeased, Rapunzel nodded as Red quickly unrolled the mapestry on the rug between them all.

"Look!" said Cinda. "The *X* is gone from the enchantress's cottage. Wait, I wonder if the crystal ball was what the mapestry — and the enchantress — wanted us to find? Maybe we weren't meant to find the treasure. Not yet anyway."

"I bet you're right!" said Rapunzel.

"Oh, too bad," said Snow. "I was really hoping for j —"

"Jewels plus gold equals treasure," her friends said right along with her. Then they all cracked up laughing.

All eyes went to the crystal ball as Red took it from the basket and placed it on top of the mapestry. The ball was still transparent and stayed that way. No pink mist swirling inside. No enchantress peering out of it.

A small silence fell among the girls and Red wondered if, like her, the others were a little puzzled. Because even though the mapestry had seemed to lead them to the crystal ball, Grandmother Enchantress now wanted them to turn it over to Wolfgang.

"Let's do a game called 'should we *give* Wolfgang the ball, or *not*,'" Red suggested. "Sort of like the 'loves me, loves me not' flower petal game."

"Give," said Red, going first. Then she gave the feathery-light ball a gentle bump with her hand. It rolled across the mapestry to Snow, who said, "Not give," before bumping it to Cinda, who said, "Give," before bumping it to Rapunzel, who said, "Not give."

They kept up the back-and-forth bumping game as Cinda emptied the basket between turns. She took out the lantern, as well as the flowers Red and Wolfgang had picked earlier that afternoon. The flowers were a bit crushed and badly in need of water by now. Skipping a few of her bumping turns, Snow got up to set the flowers in a half-filled water glass on Red's desk where she arranged them prettily.

Gazing at the flowers, Red caught the ball Cinda bumped back to her, stopping it on "give." Suddenly, she blurted, "I think I'll go talk to Wolfgang by myself." Then she grinned. "Assuming I don't get lost on the way to the library, that is!" The others laughed along with her. And they murmured in understanding when she added, "I'm guessing he'd clam up if we were all there. But I'll tell you everything he says. I promise."

As Snow came to sit with them again, Cinda spoke up. "Remember when we were all getting gowns for Prince Awesome's ball and we went into the *G* section in the library to the room where all the Grimm brothers stuff is?"

Red, Snow, and Rapunzel nodded. The Grimm brothers room was the most magical room in the whole library.

Things inside it moved under their own power. Decks of cards shuffled themselves in midair and dealt themselves out. Paperweights floated off desks and glided around the room, and books slid out from the shelves and came to rest wherever they pleased.

"I thought I saw a nose sticking through the coat of arms on the wall. Remember?" Cinda went on as Rapunzel picked up the shiny yellow braid she'd made and wound it into a knot at the back of Cinda's neck. "And later I thought I saw an eyeball?"

The other girls traded looks. "You decided you were just imagining things," said Snow.

"Yeah, because it was only your first day at the Academy," Rapunzel reminded her. "Everything was strange and new to you then. Especially magic!"

"Right, but now I'm not so sure it *was* my imagination," said Cinda.

"Hey! You don't think Grandmother Enchantress was watching us, do you?" asked Red as she began rolling up the mapestry. "Like she did from her portrait in the cottage?"

"No," Cinda said firmly. "The eyes I saw were brown and hers are gray. And the nose was way bigger than hers. But remember how she said that someone outside of Grimmlandia must be pulling the E.V.I.L. Society's strings?"

"Uh-huh, so?" said Rapunzel. She'd unwound the knot and was trying another style, piling the braid on top of Cinda's head now.

"The enchantress also said that the protective spells that keep Grimmlandia safe from the outside world are weakening." Cinda lowered her voice to a near whisper, then went on. "So maybe they're already weak enough for someone from the outside to peek in!"

Red felt goose bumps rise on her arms. Lowering her voice to the same level as Cinda's, she said, "Someone from the Dark Nothingterror, you mean?"

"Exactly," said Cinda.

Rapunzel dropped Cinda's braid. "Whoa! If what you saw was real, I wonder what it means? Grandmother Enchantress was definitely right about magic being spirited out. We all saw Peter Peter Pumpkineater's pumpkin turn into a carriage, roll into Neverwood Forest, then disappear off the edge of the mapestry. But is someone or some*thing* from the Dark Nothingterror trying to get *into* the Academy?"

Bong! The girls were so creeped out that they all jumped at the sound piping in through a grate in the wall. But it was only the Hickory Dickory Dock clock bonging the six thirty dinner hour.

"Saved by the bong," quipped Red. "Because none of us has an answer for that one!" She set the crystal ball back in her basket and shut its lid.

Rapunzel took charge of the mapestry. "My turn to guard it." After shoving it into the bag Snow gave her, she hopped to her feet. "Let's go eat."

"Yeah," said Cinda as she and the others stood, too. "One cookie just did not do it for me. I could really go for some of Mistress Hagscorch's newt's eye potpie."

"Mmm. Sounds good," said Snow rubbing her stomach.

"I'll catch you later," said Red as her three friends made to leave. "Cookie jar's empty. I want to whip up a new batch of cookies before I go downstairs. I've been neglecting my duties as Snackmaker."

"Are you sure that's a good idea?" Snow teased. "If you bake while you're hungry, you might wind up eating all the dough."

Red laughed. "I'll try to control myself."

After mixing it up, however, she couldn't help taste-testing a couple of mouthfuls. Her double-chocolate chocolate-chip cookie dough — her very own special recipe — was so good it was simply grimmpossible to resist!

Gretel came in while she was dropping the last spoon-fuls of dough into a Dutch oven, which was really just a big cast iron cooking pot. She placed it among the coals in the huge common room fireplace and then covered the pot with a tight-fitting lid.

"Mmm," said Gretel, eyeing the cookies that already sat cooling on a fresh towel atop the table. "Those smell *dee*-licious."

"Have one," said Red, nodding toward them. "But first please tell me you've had something to eat today besides cookies for breakfast and lunch."

Gretel's brown eyes twinkled as she reached for a cookie. "Believe it or not, I just had dinner."

"In the Great Hall?" Red asked in surprise.

Gretel nodded as she broke off a piece of warm cookie. "Uh-huh. My starving stomach dragged me there. I was terrified. But I kept thinking about what you said yesterday. That a person can't live on cookies. And how I shouldn't let fear keep me from eating healthy. And besides," she said with a grin, "we were totally out of cookies since I ate the last of them for lunch."

Red laughed. "Yeah. I noticed!" She thought it best not to let Gretel in on the secret of her own private stash.

Gretel giggled, then took a big bite of her cookie. "Mmm," she said around a mouthful, closing her eyes in bliss. "Anyway, since I was sooo hungry," she went on between cookie bites, "I got desperate. I decided it was up to me to face Mistress Scaryscorch — I mean, Hagscorch — in the Great Hall again."

"Yeah?" Red asked.

Gretel nodded. "My legs were like limp noodles when I entered the Hall. But I got in line with my tray anyway. I nearly lost it though, when Mistress Hagscorch handed me a plate of her special swamp stew. Because guess what she said?"

"You need fattening up!" the two girls said at the same time. Then they erupted in giggles.

"I wanted to drop my tray and run!" said Gretel. "But I was mad, too. Mad that I let her get to me like that. So I looked her in the eye and I said, 'Do I look like a stick figure to you or something? Because if I do, you probably need glasses.'"

At that, Red laughed so hard she almost fell over. "Oh, grimmtastic! I wish I could've seen the look on her face when you said that."

"Her mouth did kind of fall open," Gretel said. "But it didn't stop her from saying the very same thing to the next student in line."

Red handed her another cookie. "Here's a reward. To celebrate your courage," she said.

"Thanks," said Gretel. Then she took a few more cookies and wrapped them in a napkin. "For my brother. And for Jack and Jill," she explained. Gretel and her brother, Hansel, were best friends with the twins.

"Jack somehow managed to hit himself in the head with the magic pail this morning," she went on. "He apparently broke his crown."

"Why was he wearing a crown when he's not a prince?" asked Red.

"No, I mean crown as in the top of his head," Gretel explained. "He fractured his skull. Had to go to the infirmary and have his forehead wrapped in vinegar and brown paper. Again. He's the most accident-prone person I know. Ms. Jabberwocky had to call for the doctor and call for the nurse. They even had to call for the lady with the alligator purse."

"The alligator purse lady! Wow, Jack's injury must've been a difficult case," Red sympathized.

"Yeah, and Jill returned the pail to the library and they aren't allowed to check it out for a whole week."

As Red took the last batch of cookies from the Dutch oven, she glanced at the clock on the mantel. "Seven thirty already. Gotta run!" she said. "I haven't eaten dinner yet, and I'm supposed to be at the library by eight!"

After Gretel waved her off and headed for their room, Red left the cookies to cool on the table. An impulse seized her as she grabbed her basket. She looked back at the cookies again. Should she? Wolfgang didn't really deserve any of her precious cookies after what he'd done. Still . . .

Moving to the table she quickly piled some of the cooled cookies on top of a large red-and-white-checkered cloth napkin. Then she pulled out her magic snack-reshaping wand from her cooking tool drawer and used it to tap the top cookie on the pile.

"Your shapes instead
Shall be a wolf head!"

In an instant, each cookie on the checkered cloth magically transformed itself into the shape of a cute wolf head. Then, without giving herself a chance to change her mind, Red tied the napkin cookie bundle securely and set it inside her basket beside the enchantress's crystal ball. Slipping the basket over one arm, she wound her way downstairs to the Great Hall to grab a fig newtburger before her meeting with Wolfgang.

12

P for Puny

$\mathcal{L}$uckily, Red didn't get lost looking for the library this time. After searching along several hallways and climbing up and down many flights of stairs in search of the Grimmstone Library's special doorknob — the only one *without* the GA (for Grimm Academy) logo on it — she finally found the plain brass knob. It was in Gray Castle, the boys' side of the Academy, in the middle of the fourth floor. Strangely, it was positioned very low, about a foot off the floor.

She got on her knees and then lightly tapped the knob just as the Hickory Dickory Dock clock bonged eight. *"Honk!"* The knob morphed into the shape of a beaked goose's head the moment she touched it. "What do you get if you cross the ocean with a kangaroo?" it demanded to know. Students always had to answer a riddle before the gooseknob would let them into the library.

A kangaroo with fins? Red thought at first. But that didn't quite make sense. Hmm. The word *cross* in the riddle could have more than one meaning. For example, even though kangaroos were good leapers, no way could a kangaroo actually *cross* the ocean in a single bound. It would have to swim. So if you did cross with one, you'd get . . .

"Uh. Wet?" Red guessed in answer to the riddle.

Without another word, the gooseknob morphed back into a plain brass knob again. Which was the way you knew you'd guessed correctly. Quickly, a rectangle drew itself on the wall around the knob, becoming the library door.

This time the door was smaller than Red had ever seen it, only about three feet high and two feet wide. But as always it was decorated with low-relief carvings of nursery rhyme characters like Little Bo-Peep (running after her sheep), Jack and Jill (tumbling down a hill), and Little Boy Blue (napping under a haystack).

After turning the knob, Red crawled inside. Another strange thing about the library was that it could make itself any size it figured it needed to be on any given day. Usually it was as vast as Neverwood Forest, its ceiling as high as the treetops, with white geese flying overhead carrying books and artifacts hither and thither in nets that hung from their orange beaks.

And usually there were rows and rows of shelves stretching farther than the eye could see, and dozens of side rooms housing special collections. Like the Grimm brothers room where Cinda thought she'd seen someone peeking at her through a coat of arms.

But tonight the Grimmstone Library was even smaller than Red's dorm room! Instead of the usual enormous chandeliers, only one hung overhead, its dangly crystals touching all four walls.

A short stack of books, none more than a few inches square, and a jar holding several goose-feather quill pens sat on a ledge, which was labeled with a large ornate letter *P*. P *for what?* she wondered. *Puny?* Usually the labels in Grimmstone Library indicated what was to be found in that section of the library. And everything in here was pitifully puny for sure.

There was no sign of Mother Goose, the librarian, and certainly no geese flying by overhead. No sign of Wolfgang, either. If he *had* been here, he would've been easy to find!

After setting her basket in a corner (which was only two feet away since the area was so small), Red grabbed one of the tiny books off the ledge. There were no chairs, so she settled onto the floor of the mini-library to wait.

Good thing her friends hadn't come. No way all of them could've squished together in this small space. On the other hand, maybe the library would've expanded to hold them all? Even though this was her sixth year at the Academy, she still wasn't quite sure how the library's magic worked.

She opened the book she'd taken from the ledge. To her surprise it turned out to be an illustrated rhyme about Polly, the snippy, tea-drinking girl from her Drama and Scrying classes. Checking the spines of the other books she saw that all were books with *P* titles, like this Polly one.

In fact, this must be the entire *P*-section, she realized suddenly. Only everything had been shrunk to dollhouse size. Or *P* for Pint-size. Or small as a Pea.

Red squinted at the tiny print in the book she held and softly read it aloud:

"Polly, put the kettle on,
Polly, put the kettle on,
Polly, put the kettle on,
And let's drink tea.
Sukey, take it off again,
Sukey, take it off again,
Sukey, take it off again,
They're all gone away."

Well, that certainly explains why Polly liked tea so much, Red decided. She couldn't help it. It was part of her nursery rhyme! But who was Sukey? And why did she have to take the kettle — which was basically the same as a teapot —

off the heat? Couldn't Polly do that as well? It didn't seem like too much effort was needed to mind a kettle.

She'd just begun to wonder who "they" were — the ones who had drunk the tea and then abruptly gone away (without even a thank-you, it seemed) — when the door behind her flew open with such a whoosh that the candles in the single chandelier flickered and almost went out.

"Ow!" yelled Red. "My foot!"

"Sorry," said Wolfgang as he tried to fit himself into the cramped space. "Why is everything so small?"

"You mean *petite*, don't you?" she asked, rubbing the toes he'd accidentally stomped through her ankle boots.

He shot her a confused look, which turned to a *P* for Pained one as he bumped his head on the low ceiling. "Ow!" Rubbing his head where he'd bumped it, he sank down beside her to sit cross-legged on the floor. There was so little space in the tiny library that their knees bumped.

"Sorry," they said at the same time. Red drew her knees up to her chin under her skirt, then wrapped her arms around them.

Wolfgang chuckled, looking around. "I wanted some-place private to talk. Guess we got it, huh?"

"Which probably explains the *P*," said Red, pointing at the big *P* on the ledge. "*P* for Private! That's why the library is so small tonight!"

"Huh?"

"The entire library is just the *P* section right now," Red informed him. "Books with *P* titles. A box of *peas*. And another box of *P*s," she said, showing him a little box with *P* letters inside it. They were all different sizes and fonts.

"Well, pardon me, but this is *P* for Pathetic," Wolfgang pronounced. "We can't talk in this pint-size place."

Suddenly, an idea sparked in her head. "Hey, maybe we could *P* for Push the walls outward to make it more *P* for Pleasant in here?"

"Worth a try," said Wolfgang. They each set one shoulder against the wall opposite one another and pushed with all their might. The walls began to move farther apart, creating more room! But the pace of movement was pretty poky.

When Wolfgang's hand slipped from the wall and accidentally touched her basket in the corner, Red snatched it up and hugged it under one arm. They both stopped pushing for a few seconds, eyeing each other uncertainly. Then Wolfgang started to push again and she did, too.

"I get it," said Wolfgang. "You don't trust me because of what happened in the forest."

Red frowned at him. "What did you expect? First you steal my basket. Then you trick me into telling you stuff I'd promised my friends I'd keep secret."

Instead of responding to what she'd just said, he glanced at the basket. "I suppose you found what was inside it?"

She nodded. "The mapestry."

Wolfgang frowned. "So that's where that went. I should have guessed. But wasn't there anything else inside?" he asked anxiously.

Red arched an eyebrow. "Maybe there was and maybe there wasn't. Before we talk about that, you need to tell me the truth about why you were out in the forest. While you're at it, an apology might be nice, too."

"Or maybe just a 'pology since we're in the *P*s?" suggested Wolfgang.

Caught off guard, Red giggled against her will.

"Listen. There's stuff you're better off not knowing," he went on. "Yes, I followed you into the forest. Your story about picking flowers sounded kind of phony and I had to know what you and your friends were up to."

So Wolfgang had been afraid to trust her and her friends just as much as they'd been afraid to trust him! But was he a part of E.V.I.L.? That was the big question she wanted answered.

"Phew!" she said, huffing a breath that blew her bangs upward. "I'm *P* for Pooped. Let's stop pushing. The section's big enough that we won't be bonking into each other."

"Okay," Wolfgang agreed. As he sat again, his head

flopped forward and he let out a long sigh. "One thing I can tell you is that the enchantress is my great-great-grandmother, though," he announced.

"What?" Red's hand flew to her chest and she slid to the floor, sitting cross-legged. "But that can't be tr —" She bit off the end of her sentence as she recalled the enchantress's gray eyes, so like Wolfgang's own.

"Can't be true?" Wolfgang finished for her. "Why not? Because you and your friends have me pegged as a bad guy?"

"You did steal my basket and leave me lost in the forest," Red countered.

Wolfgang winced. "I had to get to my grandtress before you did," he told her, using what she figured must be a family nickname for Grandmother Enchantress. "To warn her you were on your way. You seemed so determined and secretive, and nobody ventures into that forbidding forest for a simple stroll to pick flowers and look at a cottage. As for why I took your basket? You might have tried to use it to magically fetch whatever you were really after!"

The *whatever you were really after* had been the treasure, of course, but they'd actually returned with a crystal ball. However, since Wolfgang didn't mention either the treasure or the crystal ball Red decided not to, either. Instead, she shook her head. "We weren't planning to *steal* anything, if that's what you mean. The mapestry directed us to her cottage."

"Yeah, but I didn't know that when I took the basket," said Wolfgang. Stretching out his legs, he crossed one over the other. "And anyway, I was only trying to delay you when I took off, not lose you. Do you think those tracks I left were by accident?"

"Muddy tracks to follow. Gee, thanks," Red said sarcastically. She set the basket in her lap and drummed the tips of her fingers impatiently on its lid. "And what about the mapestry? You took that, too, didn't you? When we got it back, there was a paw print on it."

"Sure, I took it," he admitted. "It's not safe for you girls to have it." A dark look crossed his face. "It could fall into the wrong hands."

Red glowered at him. "And you could keep it safer? Maybe you just want to find the treasure so you can keep it for yourself!" The enchantress thought she and her friends could guard it. She'd told them, too! But she wasn't ready to let him know she'd met the enchantress quite yet.

"No!" said Wolfgang. "I wouldn't . . . I mean, I couldn't . . ." His voice petered off.

"Look," Red said gently, "I believe what you said about Grandmother Enchantress being your great-great-grandmother. She must trust you. I'm just not sure *why*."

Squeezing his hands into fists, Wolfgang looked down at his lap. "Because she knows my family history."

"What's that got to do with anything?" Red asked.

Suddenly, Wolfgang jumped up, looking around as if he needed to move. "Let's *perambulate*."

"What?" Red got up, too.

"Sorry," he shoved his hands in his back pockets. "I think the *P*s are getting to me. I just meant let's walk around and talk instead of sitting."

Looping her basket's handles over one arm, Red gestured ahead. "Well, there's not really enough room to —"

Whipping around, Wolfgang set both arms against a wall of books and gave a mighty push. *Creeeak!* The wall moved and he went with it, pushing it out at least a dozen more feet. Then he did the same on the opposite wall.

When he was finished, he dusted his hands looking *P* for Pleased with himself.

"Good work." Red smiled at him and he smiled back. Then she took a step down one of the *P* aisles, and he joined her. "So what were you saying about your family?"

He shrugged. "Just that there were some pretty bad dudes in my family's past. And in the present, too. One of my uncles is even in jail for breaking and entering houses. Only he didn't *exactly* break into them. The way he tells it, he huffed and puffed and they fell right over."

"So the enchantress trusts you because there are bad guys in your family?" Red said. "That's *P* for Puzzling."

He grimaced. "No. She trusts me because she knows that becoming evil is my biggest fear. I'll do *anything* to avoid that fate!"

13

Villains and Labels

Wolfgang feared becoming evil? Seeing his pained expression, Red's heart melted for him. Suddenly, she wanted to *P* for Protect him from such a horrible worry.

"But you're *not* evil," she said earnestly as they turned a corner and started down another *P* aisle with shelves of portraits, peeping parakeets, and numerous boxes labeled 'Pithy Problems.' "I mean, you did take my basket and try to steal the mapestry, but only to help Grandmother Enchantress and keep the mapestry away from the E.V.I.L. Society, right?" Now was his chance to admit he'd tried to steal her basket to give to Mrs. Wicked.

Instead, he raised his brows. "You know about E.V.I.L.?"

She nodded. "I also know that if you were evil you wouldn't be helping Grandmother Enchantress. And you wouldn't have helped me when I fainted at the auditions, either."

Wolfgang seemed to be listening hard to what she was saying, as if willing it to be true.

She gave him a moment to let her words sink in. "So about the E.V.I.L. Society," she began. "Or maybe I should call it the *Exceptional Villains In Literature Society*?"

Wolfgang cringed. "Ugh! I hate that word *villain*. We're all fairy-tale and nursery-rhyme characters. We can't help the roles we were assigned. I'm trying to break free from that label."

"Then I'm sure you will!" she blurted. In truth, Red had never really thought about *labels* before. She'd figured all fairy-tale characters were okay with whatever role they'd been given by the author who wrote about them.

Wolfgang looked her in the eye. "Maybe you should have that same kind of faith in yourself," he said gently.

Belief in her ability to act onstage, he meant. She didn't want to talk about that *P* for Prickly subject right now. To avoid it, she propped her basket on the edge of a shelf and reached under the lid to pull out two cookies from the bundle she'd brought.

"Here," she said, handing him one. "I'm Snackmaker in my dorm, and these are my specialty. Double-chocolate chocolate-chip."

He chuckled a little as he noticed the cookies were wolf

heads. "Thanks. Nice shape," he said, taking one and biting into it. "*Mmm*." While they munched their cookies, he asked what she knew or suspected about E.V.I.L.

"I can't say," she replied swinging her basket by its handles between them as they walked on.

"Still not sure if you can trust me?" he asked shooting her a look. "That's okay. When it comes to E.V.I.L., it's hard to know who to trust. Even seemingly *good* characters can be recruited."

Red nodded. "Cinda's stepsisters tried to recruit Prince Awesome. Cinda overheard them at the ball the night she found the mapestry."

"Exactly!" Wolfgang exclaimed. "So like I said, you can't trust just anyone." He paused. "Even certain teachers."

"Like Ms. Wicked?" said Red. As they turned at the end of an aisle that dead-ended, she reached into her basket for more cookies. "I heard you talking to her yesterday," she admitted. "I was worried — I mean, I thought that meant you were part of E.V.I.L., too."

"Easy mistake," Wolfgang said wryly, nodding his thanks as he bit into the cookie she handed him. "I've been pretending to her that I'm interested in joining the Society, but just to get more information about it. She hasn't invited me to any meetings of the group yet, though."

"Meetings?" Red echoed as they turned another corner.

But inside she was jumping for joy. He'd only been pretending to be interested in joining E.V.I.L.!

He hesitated. "Listen, I know you're friends with Snow, but she's Ms. Wicked's stepdaughter, so you should be careful what you say around —"

Red blinked in dismay. "Huh? Snow is *not* like her stepmom. There's no way she'd have anything to do with E.V.I.L. And she would *never* betray our secrets to Ms. Wicked."

"Can you really be sure of that?" Wolfgang asked. "Ms. Wicked can be pretty persuasive. And even if she didn't intend to, Snow might accidentally spill a secret."

"She wouldn't," Red insisted stubbornly. But even as she defended her friend, she could feel a seed of doubt take root in her mind.

Wolfgang shrugged. "Doesn't hurt to be careful, right?" He finished off his second cookie and then brushed the crumbs from his jacket.

They turned a corner and walked down another aisle whose shelves contained pots and pans, plates and platters, potato peelers, and pastry brushes. "It wasn't very nice of you to fool me by *P* for Pretending to be the enchantress," said Red.

Wolfgang rubbed the back of his neck. "Yeah. Sorry about that. But I figured it was the only way to get you to tell me some stuff I needed to know." Suddenly, a red flush spread across his face.

Red wondered if he'd just remembered that one of the things he'd "needed to know" back at the cottage was if there was a special boy she liked at school.

"It was my accursed tail that gave me away, wasn't it?" he said quickly. "When I'm in Neverwood, it has a mind of its own."

Red laughed. She was dying to tell him that she'd found the ball in her basket, and that she and her friends had met the enchantress. But still she held back. Wolfgang was right. She wasn't quite ready to trust him.

"So why do you think Ms. Wicked hasn't invited you to any meetings yet?" she asked as they turned down yet another aisle.

Wolfgang frowned. "To become a member, I have to *P* for Prove my loyalty first."

"How?" asked Red, fearing she knew the answer.

He gave her a sidelong glance. "By stealing a magical charm or artifact and bringing it to her."

Even though she'd expected his answer, it still came as a shock. She stopped walking and took a step back from him. "You can't have my basket!" No way would she even mention the crystal ball now, much less give it to him! Surely Grandmother Enchantress wouldn't want her to.

What if he rashly handed the ball over to E.V.I.L. in place of her basket?

Pressing her charm to her chest, she folded her arms around it as if to guard it. Keeping a wary eye on him, she walked away, looking for the door out of the library.

"Wait! Listen, I had a plan, okay?" he said, following her. "Only the owner of a charm can make it work. So E.V.I.L. couldn't have used your basket to steal any magical objects or artifacts. Besides, you could've called it back or it would've come back to you on its own eventually."

"*Humpf*," she replied. She was still mad, but she slowed her footsteps, then stopped. Mulling over what he'd said, she stared aimlessly at an empty spot on the shelf across from her. "Well . . ."

Then she noticed that the empty spot on the shelf was labeled 'J & J's Pail.' "Hey!" she exclaimed. "Jack and Jill's pail is missing! Its tag isn't here, either."

There was a tag attached to everything that could be checked out of the library. You just signed your name on the tag, then left the tag on the shelf when you borrowed the item.

Quickly, Red recounted her conversation with Gretel to Wolfgang. "So after Jack's accident, Jill returned the pail here to the library," she finished. "They aren't allowed to check it out for a whole week."

Wolfgang frowned. "Which means someone else must have taken it."

"And they didn't leave the tag because they —" Red began.

"Stole the pail!" she and Wolfgang said at the same time.

"Wait till I tell Snow, Rapunzel, and Cinda!" said Red, slipping the basket's handles over her arm once more. But as she ran for the door with Wolfgang right on her heels, the library abruptly began to expand crazily in all directions, with shelves, aisles, chandeliers, and rooms popping up everywhere. The door was suddenly much farther away. It was almost like they were running toward it in slow motion!

As they came upon the *L* section, Red heard the sound of wings. *FLAP! FLAP! FLAP!* A dark shadow loomed overhead. Red looked up and heaved a sigh of relief when she saw it was only the librarian riding on the back of a gigantic snowy-white goose that was as big as a horse.

"Hello, goslings!" Ms. Goose called down to them. "Need help finding anything? I was just powering up the library. Didn't realize anyone was in here!" She wore a frilly white cap and spectacles, and a crisp white apron with a curlicue *L* embroidered on its front bib. *L* for Librarian, of course.

"We came in while the library was small," Red said, waving to her, "to talk. And we just now noticed . . . ow!"

When Wolfgang nudged her, Red broke off and looked over at him. "You don't want me to tell her about the missing pail?" she whispered to him as Ms. Goose circled.

"No," Wolfgang whispered back. "Not yet, anyway. Let's not take any chances."

Ms. Goose peered down at them, zooming closer. Straightaway her eyes went to the basket on Red's arm. "What's that?" she asked, her eyes lighting with interest.

"Um, my new charm?"

Ms. Goose swooped low to get a better look. Red gulped, as a new worry struck. *Oh, no! Was Ms. Goose going to announce that her basket was actually a library artifact?* She was the expert on such things, being the librarian and all. How disappointing it would be to find out that the basket wasn't a charm after all, and that it belonged here in the library collection. Seeming to sense what Red was thinking, the basket nestled tight to her side.

"How delightful! It *is* a charm!" Ms. Goose said after a quick inspection as she whooshed by. "And it seems to like you very much."

The basket rocked back and forth in Red's arms now, as if nodding.

"That settles it, then!" Red said happily bouncing a little on the toes of her ankle boots. "It's my charm for absolutely truly definitely sure! Thanks, Ms. Goose!"

"Let's go," Wolfgang said, pulling Red's hand as the librarian waved farewell and flew on overhead.

"Why couldn't we tell about the pail? Surely you don't suspect Ms. Goose of having anything to do with E.V.I.L.? She's so nice!" she murmured as they rushed for the door again.

Wolfgang frowned. "For now, *everyone* is a suspect. Including Ms. Goose. Who's better placed than her to spirit artifacts out of the library?"

Red could see his point, but really . . . *Ms. Goose*? It just didn't seem possible!

Unfortunately, the minute they stepped out of the library, Ms. Wicked came out of her office into the fourth-floor hallway, too. Her eyes went straight to Red's basket. From the sour look she shot Wolfgang, it was clear Snow's stepmom wasn't pleased with him. Maybe because Red was clearly still in possession of the basket Ms. Wicked wanted him to steal?

Wolfgang nodded to the teacher. "Hi, Ms. Wicked. Red and I were just practicing in the library for the play auditions on Monday."

"Is that so?" said Ms. Wicked, a calculating look on her face. "Well, I'll look forward to your performances. Mr. Thumb has asked me to help judge the auditions."

Red froze, her eyes flicking from the teacher to Wolfgang. His eyes seemed to plead with her. She wanted to deny that she was going to try out, but if she did, Ms. Wicked would know that he was lying. And that could blow his chances of getting into E.V.I.L. to spy on the group.

Do I trust him or don't I? Red asked herself. *And am I willing to face my fears and get up on that stage again?* The questions spun in her head, around and around. In a flash, the answers came to her and she spoke up.

"Grimmtastic!" said Red, looking Ms. Wicked straight in the eye. "I'll be trying out for the lead. The part of Red Robin Hood."

"Oh. How exciting," said Ms. Wicked, seeming a little taken aback by her confident tone. "Good luck to you on Monday, then." With that, she headed past them down the hall. *Click, click, click.*

Wolfgang grinned at Red. "So you're going to audition after all? Or was that little speech just now purely good acting?"

"A little of both?" she replied, grinning back. To tell the truth, she was kind of glad the decision had been taken out of her hands. Since she felt that way, it must mean that her dream wasn't quite as dead as she'd thought!

And she'd decided to trust him, right? Quickly, before

she could change her mind, she handed him her basket. "I'm giving you the rest of the cookies," she said. Then she lowered her voice and hinted, "There's something else in there you'll like, too. Something a certain enchantress trusts you to guard."

His eyes searched hers, then he smiled and nodded. "Your meaning is *crystal* clear."

"You knew we'd spoken to her, didn't you?" Red guessed. "And that I had . . . *it* . . . in here?"

"I suspected," he told her. "My grandtress can move from one place to another in ways that others can't. And also, I'd put . . . *it* . . . in your basket. But then I closed the lid. Big mistake. Couldn't get it open again. That's how I figured out that the magic must only work for you."

"Oops! That reminds me," said Red. Looking at her charm, she chanted, "A tisket, a tasket. Let Wolfgang open you *once*, basket."

Wolfgang smiled. "Thanks for deciding to trust me, Fuschia. You won't regret it. Call your basket back in fifteen minutes."

He walked off humming a tune before she could scold him for yet another nickname. Not that she would have, she thought as she watched him go. For some reason, she was starting to like those nicknames!

"Hey! Cute basket," Red heard a boy call out teasingly to Wolfgang as he walked down the hall.

"Thanks!" Wolfgang replied in a cheery voice. He didn't seem to feel the need to explain, and he didn't sound embarrassed at the teasing, either. *That's what confidence does for you*, thought Red.

14

The Fear Factor

As it turned out, Red didn't *need* to call for her basket. It appeared before her suddenly and looped its handles around her arm just as she was about to push through the white door that led into the Pearl Tower dorm.

"Back already?" she asked the basket. After giving it a pat, she peeked inside it. Good. The cookies and crystal ball were gone, which meant Wolfgang had had time to remove them before the basket had whisked its way back to her.

"What are you doing here?" Snow exclaimed when Red entered the dorm. "I thought you were going to meet with Wolfgang."

Before Red could reply, a magic feather duster flew by her nose, causing her to sneeze. *Achoo!*

Apparently, the other Grimm girls were busy at their tower tasks. In her role as Tidy-upper, Snow had just sent the feather duster flying around the room. As it began whisking along the fireplace mantel, Cinda, who was

Hearthkeeper, turned from emptying ashes into a bucket to stare at Red in surprise as well.

Red glanced at the mantel clock. Whoa! It was only 8:07 P.M.!

"Library time," she explained to her two friends as she approached them. "Wolfgang and I were there for at least an hour in normal time!" It was another peculiarity of the Grimmstone Library that when you were inside it time could either speed up or slow down. This time, time had obviously slowed down!

"So, spill," said Rapunzel. "What did you find out?"

Now it was Red's turn to look surprised. Because Rapunzel was sitting in an overstuffed blue satin chair with a scalloped back. She'd come all the way up here — again? She must not have been here long because she still appeared a little pale and shaky — the way she always looked after she climbed the stairs to the tower for a rare visit.

Red put her basket on the table and sat on a straight-backed chair beside her. Except for the four girls, no one else was in the common area. Still, Red lowered her voice since the entrances to the dorm rooms were curtains, not doors. "First off, I have bad news," she told them all. "Jack and Jill's pail is missing. Stolen probably."

"What?" Cinda set down her hearth brush, then ducked

as Snow's feather duster flew past her ear. "How do you know?"

Quickly Red told them how, according to Gretel, Jill had returned the pail to the library that morning. "Wolfgang and I were in the *P* section, and when we passed by the shelf where the pail should have been, I noticed it wasn't there."

"Maybe someone else checked it out," Snow suggested. She snagged the feather duster as it zoomed by. "That's enough dusting for now," she told it. Its feathers slumped, as if dejected — or maybe it was only pooped — as she hung it up on a hook near the fireplace.

"No," Red said. "The sign-out tag was gone, too."

"Which means the pail really must've been stolen," said Rapunzel.

Abandoning the hearth, Cinda flopped into the red velvet chair on Rapunzel's other side. "First Peter Peter's pumpkin gets stolen and now Jack and Jill's pail," she mused. "This is not good."

Snow sat down, too, perching on one of the floor cushions. "All I can say is that I hope Principal R puts his alchemy experiments on hold. Without Jack and Jill's pail, fires at the Academy will be harder to put out and way more dangerous."

"Maybe E.V.I.L. stole it for that very reason! Hoping to destroy the school," suggested Rapunzel. She turned her head to look at Red. "So what else happened? With Wolfgang I mean."

Responding to her prompt, Red described to her friends how tiny the library had been when she and Wolfgang first entered it.

"Hmm," said Cinda. "Might have been an effort to prevent more artifact thefts. Less access to the collections."

"Maybe," said Red.

Snow drummed her fingers on the floor beside her and frowned. "It would be awful if we couldn't use the library or check stuff out anymore."

It was an innocent remark that any of the girls might have made. But after Wolfgang's warning about Snow back in the library, Red found herself paying special attention to everything Snow said, alert for anything that might show she sympathized with E.V.I.L. She didn't like thinking that way at all! But Wolfgang had planted the suspicion seed in her brain and she couldn't help it.

As quickly as she could, she recounted some of her conversation with Wolfgang, revealing that she'd given him the crystal ball. Her BFFs were especially interested in what he'd said about potential E.V.I.L. Society members having to prove themselves before they could attend meetings.

"They have to steal an artifact to be a member of the Society? Hmm," said Cinda. "I bet that's what Odette and Malorette were doing when they stole Peter Peter Pumpkineater's pumpkin from the library before I came to GA! *Proving* themselves."

"Makes sense," said Rapunzel.

Snow ran a hand through her short ebony hair. "So you're saying Wolfgang *isn't* a member of E.V.I.L.? But then how did he know its rules?"

"Well, you see he —" Red stopped short. She trusted Snow, really she did. But what if Snow accidentally revealed what was said here to her stepmom? Told Ms. Wicked that Wolfgang was trying to get into E.V.I.L. just so he could spy on the group? That could put him in danger!

"He didn't say," Red finished lamely. There was an awkward pause and she could feel everyone's suspicions about him rise.

"He didn't?" Snow asked.

"Well, it's just . . . he did, but I can't tell you yet. When it's okay, I will. But I don't want to betray his trust, you know?"

"So you do trust him?" Cinda asked.

"I do now," Red said.

"Then that's good enough for me," Rapunzel said, much to Red's relief. And Snow and Cinda nodded. Rapunzel kicked off her clunky black shoes and stretched her black-stockinged legs out in front of her.

To lighten things up a little Red went on to tell them about Wolfgang's "accursed" tail that had a mind of its own. The girls all laughed about that.

"Actually," said Rapunzel, holding up one of her braids, "I know how he feels. He may have an accursed tail, but I've got accursed *hair*. It grows so fast it makes my head spin! Probably the reason I get dizzy coming up here." She gave a brittle little laugh.

The other three girls stared at her in shock. Although it was common knowledge that Rapunzel's hair grew at an astonishing rate, she was usually so touchy about it that the girls had always avoided the topic.

"But never mind about that," Rapunzel said, as if she already regretted having brought up the hairy topic. She yawned. "Time for bed."

On Monday morning, Red was awakened by a School Board announcement. "Will whoever left their silver bells and cockle shells in the Bouquet Garden last night please come to the Lost and Found to claim them?" chorused the helmet-head voices being piped through the school.

As their words died away, Red remembered it was audition day!

She threw off her red-and-white-striped comforter and scrambled down the ladder from her bed. Gretel was already up and dressed. She was standing in front of her armoire mirror brushing her hair when Red grabbed her bathrobe from a hook inside her own armoire.

"Good morning!" Gretel turned toward Red and flashed a big smile.

"Same to you," said Red. "You're sure cheerful."

"Because I slept like a rock-a-bye baby in a treetop last night," Gretel said. "I haven't had a single nightmare for two nights. I think facing Mistress Hagscorch in the Great Hall on Saturday cured me."

"Or maybe it was eating healthy food and fewer cookies," Red teased. She'd slept great, too, come to think of it. It was nice not to be jolted awake by screams in the middle of the night!

Gretel laughed good-naturedly. "Yeah, that, too."

After Red showered and dressed in the washroom a few alcoves down from hers, she brushed the snarls from her curly hair. Then she drew on a pair of red tights and threw her red cape over a yellow gown with a drawstring bodice, three-quarter-length sleeves, and a wide silk skirt.

Finally, she pulled on her ankle boots and went downstairs to breakfast.

Red's three BFFs were already having breakfast in the Great Hall. They waved when she came in and she waved back. Auditioning on an empty stomach hadn't worked out so well last Friday, so as she picked up a tray and got in line, she promised herself she'd eat more than just a few bites of something this time.

Once she was through the line, she went to join her friends. Cinda scooted over to make space between her and Rapunzel.

"Thanks," said Red as she set down her silver tray. She'd gotten a steaming hot bowl of oatsqueal, and immediately she sprinkled cinnamon and sugar on it. As she stirred the cereal around, it made a shrill sound, kind of like a cross between a badly-played violin and a whistle. Her friends were talking about moneymaking ideas again — to help keep the school afloat while they kept looking for treasure.

"Maybe we could embroider handkerchiefs and pillow-cases to sell," Snow suggested. She was sitting across the table from the other three girls.

"No way," Cinda said. "I'm totally hopeless in Threads class. I stab myself with my needle when I even so much as *think* about sewing on a button."

"Fortune-telling?" suggested Rapunzel. "We could charge a fee to read palms or tea leaves." She grinned at Red. "Or oatsqueal lumps."

Red grinned back, then swallowed a spoonful of yummy oatsqueal, which had finally stopped whistling. Like almost everything Mistress Hagscorch cooked, it had a weird name, but tasted delicious.

"I'm not sure I'd be any good at —" Snow started to object.

"Wait! I know!" Red interrupted, excitedly waving her spoon in the air. "We've come up with tons of good ideas! So what if we have a school festival with different booths and events and stuff, and use them all!"

The other three girls stared at her for a second, and then slow smiles bloomed on their faces.

"That's a *grimmazing* idea!" said Cinda, clapping in excitement. "We could invite everyone in Grimmlandia to come, and sell tickets."

"It would be a lot of work," Rapunzel mused. "But it would be worth it if it helped the school."

Snow nodded. "I bet we could get our roommates and some of the other kids here at GA to help."

"Let's keep thinking," Red suggested. "And jotting down more ideas for booths and games."

"Sounds like a plan," said Cinda. "And when we're ready we can tell Principal R about our idea. Making money with a school festival has got to be a surer thing than alchemy!"

The girls all laughed.

"Attention, scholars!" the School Board on the wall above the west balcony chorused. The students quieted and looked toward the row of helmet-heads sitting upon the carved wooden board. Visors clanking, they called out, "Please welcome Mr. Thumb."

Seconds later, the tiny Drama teacher flew into view on the balcony, riding atop Schmetterling as usual.

"Thank you," the teacher said, nodding his head to the School Board. Then he called out to the students through his thimble bullhorn. "Auditions for *Red Robin Hood* will continue in the auditorium throughout the day. All Drama class students are welcome to try out, and all non-Drama students are allowed to skip one — and only one — class period to come watch auditions."

At this news, a cheer went up in the Hall.

"Are you going to audition again?" Cinda asked Red as soon as Mr. Thumb finished his announcement. Out of the corner of her eye, Red glimpsed Snow and Rapunzel shaking their heads at Cinda.

Huh? Red had been wondering why her BFFs hadn't mentioned the auditions lately. She'd begun to think they really did doubt her acting ability and thought she should give up on the school play. But was it possible they had agreed not to talk about the subject for fear she would think they were pressuring her? *Not* because they doubted her talent?

Red considered that. It was kind of like how she, Snow, and Cinda conspired to say nothing about Rapunzel's hair or her fear of heights.

"Actually," she said, glancing around at all three girls. "I *have* decided to audition again."

"Hooray!" exclaimed Snow, bouncing in her seat with joy. "We didn't want to bug you about it, but we were hoping you'd try again."

"Can we come watch?" asked Rapunzel.

"We'd really like to be there for you this time," added Snow. "You'll be *brilliant*!"

Red smiled at their enthusiasm. "Yes, come! Friendly faces in the audience might just help calm my nerves when I step onto that stage again." She looked at Snow. "Your stepmom's helping Mr. Thumb judge."

Snow's eyes widened. "Yikes. I'll bring some stuff from my lucky collection to the audition to lend you luck."

After Mr. Thumb departed from the balcony, the

bluebirds that had been flying in and out of the Hall windows swooped down to carry the students' trays away. The birds returned with small silver bowls of water and fresh linen napkins, and the girls dipped their fingers in the water and wiped them on the napkins. Then they scraped together some toast crumbs to give to the birds in thanks. With her friends around her and a full stomach, Red was feeling pretty good right about then.

But during her first-period Threads class, she started to get nervous. Her fingers shook as she knitted a red-and-green-plaid scarf. She thought about some of the methods Wolfgang had told her he used to combat stage fright.

When Red saw that Ms. Muffet and Ms. Spider were busy helping other students and not looking her way, she set down her knitting needles. After flipping over her scarf pattern instructions, she picked up her goose-feather pen. As quickly as possible, she began to write down all of her fears about the audition as Wolfgang had advised. Then, as she picked up her knitting again, she silently read over what she'd written.

I'm afraid I might:
freeze up
forget my lines
faint again

Red's knitting needles clicked back and forth as she tried to fight her growing nervousness. If she did freeze up, she could pause and take a few deep breaths to calm down, she told herself. And she was as prepared as she could possibly be when it came to knowing her lines. Yesterday, she'd spent all afternoon in her room brushing up on them. As for her fear of fainting? She'd eaten a good breakfast, so that should help.

She set down her knitting and scribbled more fears on the list:

If I flub again, I won't get the Red Robin Hood part.
I'm afraid I'm a terrible actor.

So what if she didn't get the part? she thought. She'd be disappointed, of course. But there would be other plays she could try out for. As for being a terrible actor, it simply wasn't true. If she really stunk at acting, Wolfgang and her BFFs wouldn't have encouraged her to try out again.

Then she studied the last fear she'd written:

I'm afraid I'll embarrass myself so much that my friends won't want to be friends with me anymore.

Now that was just plain ridiculous, she thought. She trusted Rapunzel, Snow, and Cinda to be her friends no matter what. After all, she wouldn't ditch one of them if they flubbed in a big way!

Click, click went her needles as she remembered Cinda's mess-up on her first day at the Academy when she'd called out Principal R's real name in front of the whole student body. Come to think of it, that incident had actually made Red *like* Cinda — even before they'd known each other very well.

Red's friends *believed* in her. They wouldn't dump her just because she did something embarrassing. In fact, they'd probably rally around her all the more! The thought sent a burst of strength and calm through her. She only hoped it would last through third period.

15

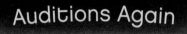

Auditions Again

"Red Riding Hood?"

It was third period and Mr. Thumb had just called her name for auditions. Instant panic set in, just like it had at Friday's audition. Red moved toward the center of the stage, her heart slamming against her chest. Her hands shook. Her legs turned to jelly. *Oh, no! Not again!*

She could see Ms. Wicked in the audience, sitting near the stage taking notes on a vellum pad. A new tremor of fear went through Red, knowing how critical Snow's stepmom could be.

Red took a couple of deep breaths. That helped a little, but she was still *s-s-scared*.

Then she remembered how Wolfgang had said that his stage fright never really went away. He'd just learned to let himself feel it, but not be undone by it.

And what about her roomie, Gretel? She'd been *terrified* of returning to the Great Hall to eat. Yet she hadn't let her fear stop her, either. She'd faced Mistress Hagscorch despite it. Gretel had survived, and Red would, too. She just needed to have faith and to *trust* herself to do her best, and that would be good enough.

"Spotlight!" Mr. Thumb yelled. The lighting crew in the control booth at the back of the auditorium was fiddling with the candelabra spotlight. They seemed to be having some trouble bringing it up.

Meanwhile, Red saw Wolfgang slide into a seat on the aisle. He'd auditioned earlier in class and had been amazing. Catching her eye now, he gave her two thumbs-up.

A few rows in front of him sat Red's three BFFs. They smiled up at her. Cinda and Rapunzel held up a glittery sign that read, KNOCK 'EM DEAD, RED!

Break a leg, Snow mouthed. That was theater talk for "good luck."

Red grinned back at her friends, relaxing some.

Suddenly, the spotlight hit her. She was ready. She positioned herself in a determined stance, opened her mouth and began to speak her lines:

"Yes, Mr. Sheriff, you're absolutely right. I'm Red Robin Hood and you've caught me red-handed!" At first her mouth felt as dry as fall leaves, but she kept going.

"Those roasted chickens in my basket *were* stolen from the king's kitchen. And I'm not a bit sorry I took them."

Feeling a sudden weight on her forearm, she looked down to see her basket hanging from her arm. She hadn't even noticed it whirl its way onto the stage. Had it come to help her out? It was the perfect prop for her scene!

Mr. Thumb hadn't said students could use props during their auditions, but he also hadn't said that they *couldn't* use them.

"These chickens aren't for me," she went on smoothly, clutching her basket that was supposedly full of chickens to her chest. "I'm taking them to people who are poor and hungry. People whose needs the king ignores." Focusing on what she was saying, she was soon completely into the character of Red Robin Hood. "Somebody has got to take care of the hungry," she declared, shaking a fist in the air. "If the king won't, I will!"

When she reached the end of her audition piece, her friends applauded wildly. She could hardly believe it was over already. She'd wanted to keep going. Because it had actually been kind of *fun*.

From his perch atop Schmetterling, Mr. Thumb called out to her from somewhere above the first row of seats. "Thank you, Red." Quickly, she took the stairs down from the stage.

"That concludes our auditions, everyone! Just a reminder that the cast list will be posted on the auditorium doors after dinner tonight," Mr. Thumb told the audience before the students began to file out of the auditorium.

As soon as she reached them, Red's three BFFs wrapped her in a group hug. "Good job, you," said Cinda.

"You were even more brilliant than I knew you'd be!" gushed Snow. She was holding a small box that Red figured contained some little objects she considered to bring good luck. And maybe they had!

"How did you like our sign?" Rapunzel asked, holding it up. "We got together in my room and made it this morning before we even knew for sure you'd audition."

Red took the sign they handed her, amazed they'd had such faith and trust that she'd manage to get through this audition. "This is so . . ." she began softly.

"Glittery?" Snow finished for her.

"Sparkly?" Rapunzel suggested.

"Grimmtastic?" Cinda added.

Red giggled. "Exactly! I love it, and I'm going to put it on the wall above my desk."

As the girls made their way to the auditorium doors Red glanced over her shoulder, looking for Wolfgang. He was by the stage talking to Mr. Thumb, but when he saw her looking at him he waved and loped toward her.

"You go on ahead," Red told her friends. "I need to talk to Wolfgang."

Snow grinned at her, and Rapunzel said, "Let's meet in the Threads classroom before we go eat lunch, while it's empty. It was my turn to guard the *You Know What* yesterday, and I've got something to show you."

"Meet you there," Red promised.

As her friends walked out of the auditorium, she and Wolfgang traded a smile. "You sounded like a pro up there on the stage," he told her.

"Thanks," she said. "Your tips really helped. I pretty much used all of them in combination."

"Glad to be of service, Rose," he said, giving her a teasing half bow.

She sent him a quick grin. Then, lowering her voice and checking to make sure Ms. Wicked wasn't nearby, she said, "About that *wicked* problem you mentioned. What if I lend you my basket again just long enough for you to score a meeting with a certain Society?"

"But I thought —"

"Ms. Wick — I mean, a certain teacher doesn't seem to know yet that it's my magical charm," Red interrupted. "So you can give it to her to show you're serious about joining E.V.I.L. But then . . ."

After she outlined her plan, Wolfgang said, "You're brilliant, Red Riding Hood, did you know that?"

Red beamed at him. "So you *do* know my name!"

They laughed, which sent a bubbly kind of happiness through her. Quickly she said bye and went to go meet her friends who awaited her in the Threads classroom.

"So how do you feel now that the audition is finally over?" Cinda asked Red when she arrived.

"Hugely glad I got through it!" Red exclaimed. "Now that I survived my stage fright once, I feel like I could do it again."

"Fingers crossed you get the part," said Snow.

"The role of Red Robin Hood is tailor-made for you," Rapunzel agreed.

"Thanks," said Red. "I'm going to be biting my nails till that cast list goes up."

Rapunzel tugged the mapestry from the black bag she was holding. "Look," she said, unrolling the mapestry on top of a desk so they all could see it. "This is what I wanted to show you."

The girls gasped. "There are new stitches now!" Cinda said in wonder.

Indeed, more golden stitches had been added onto those that had led them all to Grandmother Enchantress's cottage in the center of Neverwood Forest. Now the stitches looped back to the Academy, ending at a golden cross-stitched *X* . . . smack in the center of Pink Castle!

"What?" Red said in surprise. "Does this mean the treasure could actually be right here in the Academy?"

"Or maybe the *X* doesn't mean treasure after all," said Cinda. She sent Snow an apologetic glance for even suggesting it might not turn out to be gold and jewels.

The girls traded speculations on what the *X* could possibly indicate. Jack and Jill's stolen pail, perhaps? Some other magical object? Or was it truly the treasure itself?

"Pink Castle is huge," said Snow. "How are we ever going to find what we're looking for if we don't even know what it is?"

Red's gaze darted to Snow. She wished she could completely trust her again. After all, they were BFFs! But was Snow trying to discourage them from looking for the treasure now? She really hoped that wasn't it.

"Good question," said Rapunzel. "But we still have to try."

"And we'll have to be careful not to let anyone figure out what we're doing," Cinda said. "E.V.I.L. could have eyes everywhere."

Snow shuddered, looking around. "Do you think so?"

Quickly, Rapunzel shoved the mapestry back into her bag. "We'll only search after everyone is in bed asleep," she suggested in a low voice.

The others nodded. All a little spooked now, they hurried off to lunch.

Afternoon classes dragged by for Red, and her anxiety about the outcome of her audition began to rise again. At dinner that night she only picked at her puffy, golden shrewfflé.

"If you're too nervous to go look at the cast list, I could stay here with you while Cinda and Rapunzel check it and report back," Snow offered kindly.

"No, I'll go," Red replied. "But will you all come with me? That way you can give me celebratory hugs if I do get a role, or hugs of sympathy if I don't." She managed a small wobbly grin. "See, it's a win-win. 'Cause either way I'll get hugs."

A small group of students was already gathered around the lists after dinner as Red and her friends approached the auditorium doors on the fourth floor. Red clutched her basket and looked around for Wolfgang and Ms. Wicked. Neither was there. Not yet, anyway.

"Woo-hoo!" Red heard Polly yell. "I'm Red Robin —" At those first words Red's stomach took a dive. But then Polly finished. "— Hood's mother in the play!"

"Hey, Red," Polly yelled, seeing her. "Do you like tea?"

"Um, yeah," Red said.

"Good," said Polly, giving her a pretend evil look. "I'll bring you some during that scene where I come to visit you after you get thrown in jail."

"Thrown in jail?" Red repeated. She remembered that scene (minus the mention of tea), and if *she* was the one in jail that could only mean one thing. She craned her neck to scan the list for her name. "I'm Red Robin Hood!" she shouted in amazement. She'd gotten the lead! The part she'd dreamed of all along.

She and her friends hugged one another and jumped up and down with excitement. To Red's surprise, Polly gave her a hug, too. "This play is going to be a blast!" she said.

Red hugged her back. "I think so, too." Polly could be snippy at times, as well as tea-obsessed, but maybe there was more to the girl, Red decided now. Who knew? It might be fun getting to know her better during rehearsals.

After the girls had all calmed down a bit, Wolfgang suddenly appeared. He smiled at Red. "Congratulations, Red Robin Hood!"

"You too, Tiny John." She'd seen his name on the list. It was no surprise at all that he'd gotten the male lead role. The name Tiny John was actually a joke, though. Because the character was quite big.

He nodded, starting to say something. Then Cinda

called out, "Ready to go, Red?" She, Snow, and Rapunzel were already moving toward the staircase.

"I'm coming," Red called back. She looked at Wolfgang. Smoothly slipping her basket to his arm, she murmured, "A tisket, a tasket. Stay with him for now, basket."

She expected Wolfgang to head off then, to put the plan they'd discussed in motion. But instead he stuck around, saying, "Once the rehearsals start, we'll be practicing our lines together."

Red smiled. "Sounds fun."

His gray eyes smiled into her brown ones. "Yeah, to me, too." He reached out a hand.

Was he going to hold hers? Red's breath caught.

Then they both heard the clicking of high heels. Ms. Wicked appeared in the hallway, her eyes obviously searching for someone.

"Later, Ruby!" Wolfgang murmured, grinning at her. Then he headed for Ms. Wicked.

Red rolled her eyes, grinning back. As she moved toward her friends, she peered over her shoulder to see what was happening with Wolfgang and Ms. Wicked.

She watched him start to hand the basket to Ms. Wicked. The teacher reached for it, her eyes glinting with excitement.

Quickly, Red whispered, "A tisket, a tasket. Return to me now, dear basket."

The basket flew out of Wolfgang's hands! It scooted and twirled its way down the hallway toward Red as fast as it could go.

"Come back here!" Ms. Wicked snarled. She chased after it for a few steps, but when faces turned toward her in surprise, she quickly halted. That didn't stop her from glaring at Red as she scooped up her charm, however. A little nervous, Red backed away. What was the teacher going to do next?

However, she'd worried for nothing. With a shrug, Ms. Wicked only turned away, a forced smile on her face. Heels clicking, she went back to where Wolfgang was standing and said something to him. As he followed the teacher down the hallway, he looked over his shoulder at Red and winked.

She winked back, hoping that her double-cross plan had worked. After all, he'd *tried* to do as Ms. Wicked asked . . . or so it must have appeared to her, anyway.

"Come on," Rapunzel urged. "We need to figure some more stuff out about —"

"Yes, yes. The treasure!" Snow interrupted gleefully.

"Treasure? What treasure?" Cinda's stepsisters, Malorette and Odette, had crept up beside the girls.

Red thought fast. "The treasure Red Robin Hood steals from the king and gives to the poor. Rapunzel and Snow are making props for the play."

"Oh. Boring," said Malorette. With a sniff and a one-handed fluff of her black hair, she and Odette went on their way.

Cinda lifted an eyebrow. "Is part of being a good actor coming up with quick and convincing stories?" she asked Red. "If so, you've got that nailed!"

The girls all laughed.

As they headed off together, Red dropped back a moment as she passed the cast list posted on the wall. She smiled softly when she read her name there again.

LEAD ROLE, RED ROBIN HOOD: RED RIDING HOOD.

Hoorah! She could hardly wait for rehearsals to start. And there was also a treasure to find, and maybe a festival to plan for, too. Not to mention an E.V.I.L. Society to foil!

Hugging her basket to her side, Red gave an excited little skip and then hurried to catch up with her friends.